OPERATION LOTUS

PROMISE ME A MIRACLE
BOOK FIVE

KAREN D. BRADLEY

AMBROSIA SANDS BOOKS

Operation Lotus Book 5 of the Promise Me A Miracle Series

Each book is standalone

Published by:

Ambrosia Sands Books

PO Box 827

Dolton, IL 60419

www.ambrosiasands.com

Operation Lotus © Copyright 2023 by Karen D. Bradley

Trade Paperback ISBN: 978-1-7336089-7-8

Digital ISBN: 978-1-7336089-8-5

Library of Congress Control Number: 2024917910

Cover Art by: Woodson Creative Studios www.woodsoncreativestudio.com

Interior Design by: Lissa Woodson www.macrompg.com

◆DEDICATION◆

To all those who are facing challenges and need small miracles to bring light, love and joy into their lives.

◆ACKNOWLEDGEMENTS◆

To my family and friends and core group of readers, thanks for supporting me through the ups and downs of this writing journey. Most of what I have accomplished has been due to your excitement and encouragement that has provided fuel needed to keep one foot in front of the other.

A special shout out to my sister, Jenetta M. Bradley, for her part in getting my books off the shelf where they were collecting dust. I appreciate you reading my stories repeatedly without complaint.

English and Grammar were never my strongest subjects but the stories in my head didn't seem to care about that fact. Thanks to my editor Lissa Woodson (Naleighna Kai) for your energy and efforts in strengthening the weakness in my writing, challenging me to be better and improving the novel.

To J.L. Campbell and Debra Mitchell, I appreciate your time and assistance. Your comments, corrections and questions were essential to putting the final touches to the story.

A special thanks to J. L. Woodson for doing what you do best.

Finally, thank you to everyone who purchases a book. Know that your support is appreciated.

CHAPTER 1

"Unbelievable! Dro is moving around so much it's almost impossible to nail down a rescue plan."

Noelle Jakob glanced at her cousin as she delivered the bad news. Everything had been crazy since Dro and the father of Lola's friend hadn't made it out of Ajid—a country in the Middle East.

"He's changing locations regularly to avoid getting caught by the government and possibly killed." Mia Atwood pushed back from the desk, stretched, then continued typing.

Noelle swept her long braids over one shoulder, shot to her feet and grabbed a printout before moving toward Mia. They were in one of three temporary command centers set up in a Bella Russe Hotel's penthouse suite. "Then I should be making sure the team has whatever they need to rescue them and so they make it in time for the wedding."

She stared at Mia and tossed the picture of lotus flowers and the email printout on the laptop keys. "Not searching for these." Noelle couldn't believe they pulled her off logistics for something as simple as this.

"If you don't want to be a part of Operation Lotus, then just say so." Mia stood, glaring her displeasure. "Because there are two parts to this mission. One." She lifted an index finger. "Getting the groom and company state side for the big event." Mia raised another finger. "Two. Getting those flowers to the reception venue."

"My skills could be put to better use on the recovery team than procuring flowers." She crossed both arms over her chest, hoping her cousin would put a word in with the boss, Daron Kincaid, to return her to the original assignment.

Noelle had become close to Dro in the year she worked at Crossroads Security and met him through events at the Castle, which was a global organization with a humanitarian mission. He'd been teaching her Spanish, and now her vocabulary went beyond *hola* and *adiós*. Dro had been helping to track down her father's side of the family, which she believed were from San Miguel de Allende, the same city in Mexico the Reyes' family were from. She felt driven to do all she could to bring him home.

"Daron entrusted the assignment to me, and I gave it to you." Mia snatched the papers from the keyboard. "Did I select the wrong person?"

"No." Noelle took the documents and headed to her station, resigned to fully commit to the new project. "Please, keep me in the loop."

"This florist is the one Calvin hired for our wedding." Mia's dark-brown eyes softened as she spoke about her husband and reclaimed her chair. "From everything I heard via Lola's wedding coordinator, Kathy, Violet's on top of things. For her to drop off the map and then none of her clients have seen or heard from her in days, something else is going on."

Noelle suddenly felt bad for being so focused on Dro that she forgot he might not be the only one who needed a miracle for the holidays. "I'm on it."

She understood the importance of finding the florist, but Noelle's primary focus was the flowers. If locating the lotuses took some of the pressure off her partner so he could conduct the search, then she'd play her part. It wouldn't stop her hunting for a loophole to get back to the original duties. Noelle was hoping if she could find the lotus flowers for the reception, then maybe she could convince Mia to leave her partner to find the florist on his own.

"The quicker you take care of this, the faster you'll be back on the logistics team." Mia's focus went back on the screen.

Noelle tried to take Mia at her word but wondered if her cousin couldn't see past the girl who was always in trouble and making the wrong choices, to the woman she'd actually become. Uncle Mason had convinced Mia to give her this chance, and she was determined to make her family proud for once. No one but her uncle knew she used to run illegal merchandise for her ex-boyfriend, Rafael, through a global network and almost landed in prison. Noelle was glad her uncle set her straight and kept it out of the family rumor mill.

She shook off the past and tackled the list of flower shops first. After seven failed attempts to locate what they wanted, she scoured the internet. When the online floral results were a casket arrangement and a bouquet with orchids, not lotuses, she realized tracking down the florist may be the quickest solution to getting back on logistics where the real action happened. She shot off a message via the company chat app to Zane Hargrave, the man she'd partnered up with for this task, to see if he'd found anything. He replied saying he was following a lead.

Noelle noticed the report didn't say if someone else was working in the floral shop. Or whether it was open. She dialed the number on file.

"Hello this is Harris at A Sacred Heart Flower and Gifts. How may I help you?"

"What are your hours of operation?" When he replied, she jotted down his name and information on a sticky note and said, "Thank you."

Noelle slipped the phone into her pocket, then grabbed her coat, purse, and boots from under the desk. "I'm going to talk to the floral assistant to see if I can get better answers face to face."

Mia glanced over her shoulder. "I'll be going to The Castle to help Calvin with some amendments to certain gear we'll need to get Dro home."

"Tell your hubby, I said hola." She scanned the desk to make sure she hadn't left anything she'd need, then peeked out of the master bedroom. The hallway was empty, so she dashed into the entertainment room down the hall, past the other bedroom where another workstation was setup until she made it into the living room's foyer.

"Jingle Bells."

That name was the first sign she hadn't made a clean escape.

"You're not leaving without me, are you?" The six-foot muscular man with captivating dark-brown eyes jogged towards the door.

"Sí. Heading to Sacred Heart Flower shop."

"Holly." He glanced down at her and scowled. "You're not a team player."

The man called her everything but her name. She had become tired of trying to correct him. Noelle tried her best not to roll her eyes as she slipped off her indoor shoes and put on a pair of boots and winter gear. "Zane, you're responsible for tracking down Violet."

"As a team we're …" He waved a hand between the two of them. "… supposed to work together to handle both."

Noelle frowned. Zane was sexy as hell for a man with shoulder length hair, which wasn't her thing, but he annoyed the mess out of her. "I thought you were researching something."

"I was, which is why I came to find you." He grabbed a winter vest off the coat rack.

Noelle opened the door, heading to the elevator. Without glancing over her shoulder, she could feel him following her.

"I asked myself ..." He stuck an arm in the open elevator, allowing her to enter first before stepping in and using his keycard to press the parking level reserved for Crossroads Security. "... Could there be a legit reason besides a lost phone that would cause our florist not to pick up when her people called?"

"And what answer did you come up with, Einstein?" She took in his strong jawline, hating and loving how her senses always came to life any time he was near. The sensual, spicy scent coming off him tickled her nose. Noelle hadn't been attracted to an Asian man before, but like a heat-seeking missile Zane drew her in from the first moment she saw him. Whenever he was in a room she couldn't stop checking him out, which was why she tried to avoid him. The last thing she needed was a work relationship to go wrong and lose the ground she gained with her family, and in her career.

He retrieved a set of keys from a vest pocket. "I checked to see if there were any cell tower outages with her provider near the flower shop or her apartment building, but there were none."

Noelle made a mental note to check the morgues on the way to the flower shop. No one wanted to go there yet. She hoped she wouldn't have to deliver any bad news.

Zane gently guided her away from her Hyundai Elantra to the company issued Lexus NX.

"Excuse me. You're the ride along. Not me." Noelle turned, heading toward the Elantra.

He chuckled. "If you wanted to be the driver, then you should have signed out a company vehicle."

"We're only going to a flower shop." Noelle put a hand on one hip preparing to stand her ground.

"A woman has gone missing." Zane tilted his head and frowned as though she'd lost her mind. "This is not a normal flower run, Holly."

Noelle huffed as he nodded to the passenger side of the Lexus. "Fine. I hope you're better at following GPS than you are at remembering names."

CHAPTER 2

This new assignment caught Zane off guard. Everyone was monitoring Dro's movements to find an opening for a rescue. When Zane found out they partnered him with Noelle, he felt the universe had granted him a holiday wish. This would be the first time he didn't have to work hard to get her attention. During this limited opportunity, he wanted to find out if his pull towards her was only physical attraction or something deeper.

He glanced at Noelle's golden-brown face while she focused on the phone sitting on top of a notepad as she made calls using a low tone. He wondered if the person on the line could hear her when he was sitting next to her and couldn't make out what she was saying. Noelle crossed something off the page filled with as many small drawings as words. She didn't notice they had arrived at their destination.

"We're here." He turned off the engine and grabbed his phone from the console.

"Dios mío. That was quick." Her honey-brown eyes shifted with laser-like focus to the building storefront that had large,

7

framed windows and a black awning. "Are you upset that this side mission might keep you off the extraction team?"

"Things will work out as they should." Zane had mixed emotions about it, but he would not tell her that. Daron and Nicco were already headed to Durabia. They planned to slide secretly into Ajid and meet up with Dro to explain the tentative escape strategy, which required on-the-ground planning. If it was just extracting Dro, this would be easy, but there was a lot more at stake. The second team was due to fly out soon with the equipment, weather permitting. If Zane wasn't on that plane, he'd be disappointed not to be a part of the rescue mission. On the other hand, his family would be relieved he was somewhere safe for the holidays. His assignments caused them many anxious moments.

"Let's hope."

"What had your attention on the drive over?" He unbuckled the seatbelt, shutting down the urge to get out and open her door knowing he wouldn't do it for a male coworker.

Noelle removed the restraint from across her ample chest. "Making sure the florist hasn't turned up in the morgue." She slid out of the truck, waiting for him on the curb. "She has not. Maybe once we leave, we should make sure she wasn't admitted to the hospital."

His eyes lowered to the form fitting jeans, appreciating all her lovely curves. The peach jacket stopped at her waist and showcased a coke bottle shape that commanded attention. He was glad Daron didn't have any rules against dating coworkers. Regardless, he'd learned over time that sometimes sexual harassment was subject to each person's interpretation. A simple compliment could be seen as just that by one woman and sexual harassment by the next. Until Noelle gave him the green light, he wouldn't make a move. While she hated when he didn't call her by her name, over the last few months it had been the only way to catch her attention.

"I'll shoot off a text to Roc," he said, almost getting caught checking her out when she frowned at him as if to say, *are we going in?* "He can look into hospitals while we're here." The team was concerned for Violet but one thing that comforted them was the evidence pointed to her leaving of her own accord, at least so far.

"Good idea."

They fell in step, heading to a glass door with black wood frame. Through the windows, flower arrangements in black planter pots sat in each panel. He held the door open for her before he could catch himself.

Noelle gave a warm smile as the door chimed when she crossed the threshold. "Gracias."

A floral scent surrounded them in its welcoming embrace. The first thing he noticed was an exposed brick wall and a black insert with the shop's name written in white behind a counter covered with red roses.

"I can't believe they didn't already order the flowers with the event being less than two weeks out," Noelle whispered as a man with a name tag that said Harris greeted them.

Zane shot off the text to Roc as they approached the stylish slender man. He wore a pink shirt with designer jeans and was busy gathering rose petals

She smiled sweetly. "I'm following up to see if Violet has updated you on the lotus flowers for the Reyes and Samuels wedding?"

"I'm sorry to say." The man continued bagging petals, but put his gaze on them. "No one has heard from her in three days."

Zane moved closer to the long counter. "When was the last time you talked to her?" The report already had the man's statement, but people sometimes gave a little more detail with every retelling.

"Shortly after we wrapped up our last wedding." He placed a bouquet of red roses on the back counter, along with the bag of petals. "Once we confirmed we had set everything up to the coordinator's liking, I told her I'd do one last check, then leave."

9

"Did she say anything to you?" Zane eyed the security system and noticed several cameras aimed at the door, the register, the back room near the black spiral stairs to the upper level, and another one to catch most of the activity in the main area. A few more cameras were probably situated upstairs.

"Just that the next few weeks would be crazy. She had a special order of flowers that she'd take extra care to make sure were beautiful for the event and that she'd catch me up on the Reyes' wedding the next day since the date had been pushed back again." Harris glanced at the door as it chimed. "Her phone rang, she said goodbye, then walked away to answer."

Maybe Violet's problem was more of a personal nature. "Was she having issues with anyone lately?"

"We had a couple that she refused to work with, who were harassing her to take them on as clients. A few of our flower shipments were also stolen and left on the side of the road." He placed an index finger to his temple and his eyes lifted toward the ceiling for few seconds. "Other than the couple and the person behind the thefts, I can't think of anyone else who had a problem with her."

"Was she at the shop the next morning?" Noelle asked.

"Usually she's the first one here, but I had to open the shop that day. She hasn't answered my calls, or come in since." He smiled and held up a single finger to the customer lingering near the refrigeration unit close to the spiral stairs. "I called her daughter, but Paige was overseas on a photography gig. When Paige finally reached out, she said she'd have the police do a wellness check. According to her, Violet left a message saying she was extremely tired and would be resting, so not to worry if she didn't get back to her immediately."

The male customer's eyes stayed on the trio and he barely glanced at the floral arrangements surrounding him. *Was he really there for flowers?* "Why didn't she let you know she was feeling under the weather?" Zane asked, returning to the conversation while monitoring the new arrival.

"That's the reason Paige requested a wellness check, she was scared Violet was sick and didn't want anyone to know." Harris cleared the rose stripper, scissors, and other items off the countertop before rounding the corner onto the sales floor. "Let me take care of this customer. I'll be right back."

Noelle studied Harris carefully. "Did you check to see if there's been a missing person report filed for her with the police?"

Is she thinking what I'm thinking? Could Harris have a vested interest in Violet not returning to the shop?

"The daughter filed one today." Zane glanced at the camera behind the counter. Roc ordered them to avoid getting in the police's way while they investigated. Zane's plan to check out Violet's apartment changed because of that. "I wonder if Harris even thought to confirm whether she returned to the store after the wedding."

"We need to visit the location of the last wedding." She whipped out her phone just as Zane's vibrated in his pocket. "Maybe there's footage to give us a better timeline on her movements."

He opened the link in the text, reading the article as Noelle searched for the address of Violet's last known location in the file, though he'd already committed it to memory. Zane would obtain the security footage from the flower shop that night.

"Nelly. Our florist may have witnessed an abduction." He handed Noelle the phone. The incident mentioned in the news story occurred shortly after the last time Harris spoke to Violet. "Her last call happened in the estimated window during which a businessman went missing from a condo across the street from the venue."

CHAPTER 3

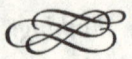

"*A* prominent businessman, Jermaine Chamberlain went missing over the weekend, shortly after leaving his condo. The police suspect foul play."

Noelle peered at the cell phone as the newscasters showed a video of the man leaving a building and walking into the dimly-lit street.

"His family is asking for anyone in the community, who has information, to come forward. A cash reward is being offered for any tips leading to his location or the arrest of the people who may have taken him."

The news reporter mentioned he'd been a positive influence in the community and had spearheaded a plan to build a new outreach center. Noelle left the site when they cut to a pre-recorded clip of the wife crying and pleading for his safe return with their two children attached to her side. Noelle wondered if the changes he was making in the community were too positive for someone's liking.

She was sure some dangerous men had taken him if the footage of Violet running back into the hotel across the street from Chamberlain's building and rushing to the parking garage was any indication. Unfortunately, the hotel camera covering the area outside the ballroom window to the corner was being serviced and didn't capture the incident.

Raising her key to the door sensor, she entered the suite and slipped cloth booties over her shoes this time instead of taking them off. She was scheduled to speak with the wedding coordinator and wouldn't be there long.

Her cell rang and her friend Shanay's name appeared on the screen. "Is everything okay?" Noelle asked, almost in a whisper. The penthouse seemed quiet, but most of the team were reviewing the latest mission updates or submitting them.

"Did I catch you at a bad time?" Shanay inquired.

"No." Noelle passed through the living room area. "I'm not used to you calling so early unless it's an emergency, or something crazy." She flipped on the light, entering the workspace in the master bedroom.

"If telling you to keep your head on a swivel is something crazy, then this qualifies. Word on the street is your ex has been seeing a lot more visitors lately and there's a rumbling about getting the old gang back together."

Noelle stayed near the door to watch for anyone entering the office. The last thing she wanted was someone overhearing the conversation. "That's not good."

"I need to go but I should have more info before we meet for drinks." Shanay disconnected the call before Noelle could respond.

The two of them were the only ones who had worked with her ex-boyfriend who went straight after avoiding prison. Noelle hoped like a person driving with the gas tank on E, trying to make it to the gas station, that her past wasn't about to destroy the life she'd built. Noelle approached her desk, which held a gift box with white sparkly snowflakes and a red ribbon. "What's this?"

She scanned the area to see if anyone was standing in the doorway. Mia was at the daily stand-up meeting receiving intel on the other ongoing operations. Who knew a mission to find the bride's friend, Alia, and invite her to become the maid of honor would spiral into other operations? They ranged from finding out what caused the catering staff to fall ill, getting the custom rings to Chicago, to repairing the wedding dress—which was a family heirloom. Of course, the biggest mission that developed was getting the groom along with Alia's father to America for the big day.

A slight rapping on wood caught Noelle's attention as she set the only designer purse she owned down on the desk.

"Nelly, Kathy postponed your meeting," Zane said. "Roc and Linc are handling the search for Violet today. I'm free to help you with the lotuses."

"Really?" Noelle pursed her lips. "How?"

"Mr. and Mrs. Moneybags have a meeting to see the speakeasy ballroom in twenty minutes." Zane leaned inside the threshold wearing a grey tailored suit and a baby blue shirt with no tie. His hair was pulled into a neat ponytail at the nape of his neck. She felt a little underdressed in a simple but elegant black sweater dress.

"Give me ten minutes and I'll be ready." Noelle waved him off then logged into the computer.

Zane walked over, laying a pendant on the desk, which was part of their surveillance equipment and contained a tiny camera.

. "You'll be needing this for our outing." He smirked as he left.

As she waited for the authentication text to come in, she opened with an index finger, the red little card attached to the gift.

Be as resilient as a lotus. As long as your roots are firmly planted in who you are, you can endure extreme circumstances and still bloom. Your secret Santa.

Noelle opened the box to find a crystal lotus flower. In her research she found out, as long as its roots were firmly planted in the water or mud, it could endure extreme conditions. At least that's what one article said, another contradicted that fact slightly, but she was choosing positivity today.

"Mia." She smiled, placed the gift on the desktop, snapped a picture then sent her cousin a text with the image and the message, *it's beautiful*. Her finger traced the crystal petals as she pondered what about this gift made her morning.

Glancing at her watch, she decided to review her emails on the ride over to the hotel. She dialed a number, putting it on speaker. "Roc, did you find any flower shop footage?"

"Seconds from sending you and Zane the video clip." Roc paused, and his fingers tapping the keyboard echoed from the other end. "It seems your girl hit the floral shop's safe before pulling a Houdini."

"Good to know. Gracias." Noelle checked the time again, grabbed her purse and made a few steps before crashing into a solid mass. She stumbled back.

"Jingle Bells. You okay?" Zane steadied her with both hands.

"I was until I crashed into the brick wall called you." Noelle failed to mention the contact had nerves in her body singing in three different languages; longing, desire, and lust. That spicy cologne she loved, filled her nostrils and interrupted her attempt to regain her composure.

"Maybe pay attention to where you're going and that wouldn't happen." He smirked, shifting her to the side as another coworker entered the hallway.

Noelle stepped around Zane the moment the hall cleared, heading to the exit. "I assume you were looking for me for a reason."

"Would you be fine flying solo for a half day?" Zane followed, waving as they passed the open bedroom door operating as a secondary office space for three other personnel, and exited the penthouse behind her.

"Why?" Noelle slipped off the shoe booties on the elevator ride down to the car.

Zane scanned the area before unlocking a Rolls-Royce Cullinan. "I let some personal things slip through the cracks and need to handle them before I go overseas."

"Which will not happen unless we get a lead on the missing florist. And we're not having too much luck finding these lotuses."

"We might have one," he countered.

"*If* we can get our potential new florist a picture of the ballroom space to create prospective arrangements *and* work some logistical magic to have them here in a week."

Noelle had agreed they needed to identify an alternate location to get the lotus flowers. Harris confirmed the flower order for the wedding ceremony last night, but not the reception.

She chuckled as they drove around the back end of the hotel to the private parking lot for the basement bar and ballroom.

"If you plan to do some follow up with the florist, just let Roc know and he'll go with."

Noelle had no intention of doing that. If this meeting went well, she planned to spend the rest of the day watching news reports to stay up to date on what was going on in Ajid and working on her own private project. She wanted to know where all the hospitals, aid stations, and checkpoints were in case anything needed to change on the ground.

Her assignment on the logistic team was to work out the worst-case scenarios. She was building an interactive three-dimensional map that allowed her to alter and update data quickly. The only new information out of Ajid was a report on an earthquake damaging a village near Dro's last reported location. If things didn't go well, she would focus on figuring out the next move regarding the lotuses instead of her normal evening routine.

She looked at his glasses. "I can't believe we have to use spy gear to get photos of the venue."

"Man listen, when the team had to create a high-profile alias just to get the appointment … my mind was blown." Zane entered a code and the parking garage door opened. He pulled into the reserved spot, then grabbed a pair of glasses from the console, hopped out and rounded the car, and opened the glass door for her.

"Welcome. I'm Eden." The slender brunette sported a navy Versace suit. "I'll be giving you the tour your wedding coordinator requested."

Noelle followed her and was surprised by the lackluster basement decor. The area had a high ceiling and tiled floor with a hallway wide enough for two cars to drive next to her. "Thank you."

"Is this it?" He scanned the space as they slipped into the golf cart waiting by the wall across from the entrance.

"We bring our potential clients to this entrance to show how their vendors would get in." She drove down the long hall, stopping at the end. "The double doors to the left is the vendor's entrance. I'll be taking you through the guest entrance." She stepped up and opened a single door.

Noelle removed her coat and laid it in the cart to make sure the camera pendant on her dress wasn't blocked. She adjusted the pendant to activate the camera, fully aware that Zane's glasses were recording their entrance. Mia would not approve of them using Crossroad Security equipment to break the rules with Dro's reception destination.

"As you know, we do not allow picture or video. Once you sign the contract, your vendors will be given all access to our floor plan, virtual viewing space and have appointment only access to the room prior to the event as long as they sign the NDA."

"We understand." Zane slid his arm around Noelle's waist as he crossed the threshold.

Noelle's body temperature spiked immediately as they went from the carpeted area to another set of glass doors. The bar section was enormous, elegantly decorated with a beautiful iron rail door which gave a perfect view into the wine cellar. She led them through the assorted bottle displays to two arched wooden doors.

Eden opened the entry and finally gave them a genuine smile

that brightened her lovely features. "This is where the magic happens."

"This is amazing." Noelle's eyes immediately went to the three lotus flower ceiling lights.

"A pool." Zane's gaze went to the private bars on opposite sides of the entrance before moving forward. "That, I did not expect."

"Isn't a pool a safety hazard at a wedding?" Noelle angled her body in the direction she wanted the camera to record.

Eden walked backward to the pool. "It hasn't been a problem."

Zane reached for her as Eden took a step that would land her in the water. "Careful."

"Thanks for the concern. We have a covering on it." She turned and stepped on the water.

"Very nice." Noelle finally noticed the clear pool cover.

"This was specially made for this facility, and we've used it as a dance floor as well." She led them into the center. "It has weight sensors so that the assigned banquet manager and the event coordinator, and whoever you authorize, will get a warning if the limit is exceeded."

Zane and Noelle shared a glance. "So our guests are not allowed to take pictures?" Noelle couldn't imagine someone not taking a photograph.

"They can, but can't hashtag, mention the hotel, or turn their location on." Eden pulled up photos on a phone, showing them to Noelle. "For every client we transform the space in unique ways which makes it hard for competitors to duplicate the space. It's truly about the safety of our clients and their guests. We don't want them tracked. If you desire your guests to post freely on social media, this is not the room for you."

"Our guests will be fine with that." Zane took Noelle's hand in his, then planted a kiss on her cheek. "Right, sweetheart?"

Noelle nodded, while her heart raced as if she had sprinted across the room.

The sales manager pointed out different areas of the ballroom and explained how they were used. Eden led them into a gaming lounge with pool tables, darts, and other games, some virtual. "We have an approved vendor list but if you want to you use your own, we have the right to deny them access if they fail to meet our quality check."

Their back-up plan was slipping through the window into the ether. "How long does that normally take?"

"Three to five days depending on the vendor." Eden handed her a document.

Noelle glanced at Zane to see if he shared her concern, but his face was glued to the phone. "If we have a last-minute incident and lose a vendor, can we purchase from an unapproved vendor and have our coordinator bring it in?"

"It depends on the coordinator," Eden answered.

Noelle listened as she explained the insurance specifications while Zane's fingers tapped out a text message. "Could you give us a moment?"

"Sure." She maneuvered around them, aiming to walk into the wine cellar.

"What's going on?" Noelle whispered, noticing Eden stayed where they were in her line of sight.

"Harris gave Violet's daughter my information." Zane handed her the phone. "The daughter said someone named Smokey is searching for her mother."

Noelle returned the phone to him. "I'm surprised Paige didn't want to meet today to talk."

"Let's wrap this up and see what we can find out about this Smokey until we meet the daughter tomorrow." Zane waved Eden back over.

Noelle knew all attempts to find another lotus flower vendor would happen between searching for Violet. Their first priority was to find Violet before she turned up dead somewhere.

CHAPTER 4

"*I won't tell if you don't tell.*"

Zane chuckled at what Mia said to him yesterday about the crystal lotus flower. Being sneaky around trained security personnel was difficult, but his interest in Noelle was obvious to everyone else except her. Zane guessed Mia had already mentioned her suspicion by the way Noelle had been looking at him strangely all day. He debated whether he had thrown Noelle off when his work buddy delivered another Secret Santa gift when he wasn't in the office. Zane wanted a little mystery to remain around the gifts for now.

"What made the daughter suspect this Smokey person?" Noelle asked as they approached the porch of a brick townhome.

Zane pushed the video doorbell. "We're about to find out."

The door swung open, and a tall, brown-haired, slender woman appeared in the opening. "I'm Paige, Violet's daughter. Do you have a business card and ID?"

He pulled a wallet from his jacket pocket, retrieved a card along with his work identification badge and handed it to Paige.

Paige looked at the card, then slipped it in her back jean pocket.

"Sorry about that. I needed to confirm your identity." She stepped back, opening the door wider. "Thank you for coming."

"You're welcome." Noelle handed him a pair of boot covers.

Zane allowed Noelle to enter first as he committed the license plate of the suspicious vehicle two houses over to memory. He could have sworn he'd seen that same car at the flower shop.

He slipped the blue cover over his boots, grateful Noelle had been thinking ahead. Shoes were lined up next to an empty basket and one with individual packaged socks in various sizes. Their host wore house shoes.

Paige locked up and led them into a cozy, upscale living room with a wall of beautiful photos from across the globe. Some of those places he recognized from family trips. Zane's parents had taken him and his siblings on educational excursions all around the world, exposing them to different cultures.

He lowered himself next to Noelle onto the peach couch underneath the photo galley as their host sat in a navy chair. "Tell us about this Smokey."

"I stopped by my mom's place and the neighbor said someone offered him money to let him know if he sees her." She retrieved a sheet of paper from her pocket and handed it to Noelle.

Noelle scanned it, then handed him the note. It contained a number and the message that Smokey would pay well for any and all information from the time Violet went missing, and the day after. Any recent sightings notifications could also be converted to cash. Zane's mind automatically went to Lloyd, the one hotel employee who had avoided speaking to their people. Had he gotten a similar offer?

"Harris gave me your information. He said you were hired by the Reyes Wedding party and were connected to The Castle and could be trusted."

She was right about the Castle. Zane wasn't a member, but the owner of Crossroads Security, Daron Kincaid, was one of the Kings of the Castles. They called him King of Morgan Park and his company provided security for the organization. Only in the last year had Zane earned the right to work at The Castle. Sitting more comfortably on the seat, he said, "He is correct."

"My cousin, Mia, married Calvin, the Knight of South Holland and your mother was their florist." Noelle gave her a brief break-down of the Castle into Kings, Queens, Knights, and Ladies and how they were named after the communities they lived in or where they were doing humanitarian work. "They invest in people. Mia pulled me off another assignment to look into your mother's disappearance."

"Do you have something else?" Zane doubted she brought them here just to give them the same information she had already texted.

Paige moved from the chair, picked up a square wicker box from the floor and placed it on the table. "When I'm out of town, my mother comes over and puts all my mail in this box." Her eyes teared up as she lifted the lid. "I found a Christmas present, an envelope, and a card." She pulled the items out and handed Zane the card.

He read the contents, which definitely sounded like she was in hiding and scared that trouble might show up at her daughter's door. "We'll try our best to get your mother home for the holi-days." Zane passed the card to Noelle.

"I hope so. Her sister is flying in from Germany tonight to surprise her at our family gathering but..." She squeezed the present to her chest with her thin lips trembling.

Zane felt for Paige. Family was important to him. His biological parents left him in a fire station in a smalltown in central Illinois when he was a baby. The social services worker's home caught on fire while she was out shopping, burning the only connections to his birth parents which was a note that included his birth date, eating habits, and a request to keep him safe, along with a family photo. His adoptive parents had given him a diverse family he

22

loved with all his heart and couldn't imagine not having one of them around.

Noelle stood and dropped the card into the box, then wrapped an arm around the woman's shoulder. "Once we find her, she'll know she's not in this alone and can come out of hiding."

"If she calls you, make sure you tell her that." Zane gently guided the two women back to the couch. "You could be the key to helping us track her down. Tell us where she likes to go, things she likes to do."

For the next hour, they discussed Violet's habits and hobbies.

Noelle called and confirmed the doorman Lloyd, who was working the night Violet went missing, was on duty. On their way to the Hotel Alondra Rose, Zane noticed a sedan following them minutes after they left the house.

"This is not the way to the hotel," Noelle said as he turned left off the designated route.

Zane glanced into the rearview mirror. "I'm making sure we don't have unwanted guests."

Peering at the side mirror, Noelle said, "It seems we do."

Zane sped through a yellow light and the sedan ran the red. "I guess they're done trying to be discreet," he said as he weaved through the traffic. "Hold on."

Noelle grabbed the dashboard as he spun the car in an unexpected U-turn that had her sliding sideways. "I'd like to make it there in one piece," she yelled over the honking from the other drivers.

"We will." He took a quick right, then pulled into a parking lot.

After waiting ten minutes, he drove to the hotel by an extended route to make sure they didn't regain their tail.

Parking up the street from the Hotel Alondra Rose, Zane glanced at the door next to the ballroom entrance where the florist stepped out to accept the call. He was sure Violet had witnessed the kidnapping. His problem was the hotel camera only covered the doors and not the entire front of the building. Violet had stepped out of the camera's range for a few minutes before dashing back inside the hotel.

The doormen stood on either side of the entrance as they approached the hotel. Zane felt a death grip on his arm and realized that Noelle had slipped on a patch of black ice. The weather was warm one day and freezing cold the next, which increased the chances of ice patches on the sidewalk.

As they drew near, Zane's focus went to Lloyd, a lanky man with a baby face.

"Let's not tell him who we are," Noelle suggested as Lloyd hailed a cab for a couple.

"Good idea." He threaded his arm through hers, receiving a smile from Noelle as they approached the young man.

"Welcome to Hotel Alondra Rose." Lloyd reached for the door handle.

Noelle scanned the street, then said, "We're actually here to speak with you."

The young man frowned, releasing the door. "For what?"

"To see if you can provide Smokey with any other useful information." Zane shifted and placed his back against the wall so he had a better vantage point of the hotel lobby as well as up the street. Noelle was faced the opposite direction so she'd catch anything coming up behind him.

"I wish. Like I told the other guy…" He opened the door for a guest exiting the hotel. "…I saw her later that night on the expressway when I got off work and she was heading toward I-94W. At least, that's what I assume. I had to get off a stop before the split to pick up a friend who was riding with me to Gurnee."

"We wanted to make sure you didn't remember anything new," Noelle said.

Zane didn't like the idea of Smokey having this information and possibly a head start on locating Violet. What other information had they acquired? How close were they to finding her?

CHAPTER 5

"*D*o you think he's dead?"

Noelle waited for Zane to answer via the earpiece as she drove into the small parking lot of a bar called Clozer in the suburbs that Smokey's crew frequented. In front of a cement block building with dark windows, a few people stood with no coats on, shoulders to their ears smoking cigars.

"Who? Chamberlain, the businessman?" Zane asked.

"Sí. Maybe that's why they're so determined to find her." She backed the car into the only remaining cleared-out space. "It's obvious since Violet is in hiding, she's not planning to turn them in to the police."

"They can't be sure of that." Zane honked, which was to the signal to their backup that he was almost there, and she would be go in. "They can't risk leaving a witness."

Noelle slid out of the driver's seat and walked across the icy pavement to enter the bar. She was slightly surprised that it wasn't the hole in the wall she visualized based on the rough concrete exterior. Black leather booths, several pool tables, and a small dance floor were more upscale than expected. The bar was spruced up with a green garland with red and silver ornaments and white lights hanging from end to end. A small Christmas tree sat on the shelf next to premium liquor. The area near the pool table had assorted sizes of red, green, and black ornaments hanging from the ceiling with a Kwanzaa candle sitting in a nearby window.

As Noelle grabbed an empty stool, she noticed a back room decorated in silver and blue. Noelle was shocked that the bar had encouraged diversity in the holiday celebrations, considering the crowd that frequented the place. She had to laugh at her thoughts. When she was out in the world making mischief, she had still celebrated holidays. Most of them, anyway.

"I'm running plates now."

Zane's voice snapped her out of her thoughts. After ordering a beer from the young bartender, Noelle turned, put her back to the bar, then scanned the room. Holiday music played in the background as people milled about. "I don't see them." She made sure the braids hung over her face as she spoke to Zane.

Not even a second after she said those words, a group of men entered and headed toward the pool tables. Another set of men, already involved in heavy play, moved away and gave the newcomers their space.

"I think his crew is here." Noelle swiveled around.

The bartender cleared his throat. "That'll be three dollars."

She focused on the bartender as he opened a Corona and placed a lime wedge on the bottle's lip. "Gracias." She laid the money on the counter with a tip.

"De nada."

The bartender saying *you're welcome* in Spanish reminded her of the second secret Santa gift, which was three vouchers for conversational Spanish events. She already picked the ones she wanted to attend in the new year.

"Be there in a second." Zane's sexy voice filled her ear again, sending a delicate tingle through her body. "Just getting the license plate number off the new arrival."

Two of the newcomers made a physical sweep of the entire floor before settling near the pool table. The brother about six feet tall with dark-brown skin, took a seat in the back corner. The way they scanned the room and made an overall assessment of the people, she had no doubt these were their targets.

One tall, thick, muscular biker chick advanced toward a husky Caucasian guy. As she approached, he rose from his seated position on the stool and crossed his arms. Standing around five foot ten, she towered over him by three inches. "Are you going to give me a chance to beat you in pool finally?" she asked, playfully pulling her hair over her right shoulder.

He shook his head, then lowered himself back onto the stool, dismissing her with a wave.

The woman's ivory skin brightened to a light shade of pink as she strutted past the pool table and sitting area, then claimed a space next to Noelle. She ordered a Miller Genuine Draft but didn't acknowledge Noelle. Obviously licking her wounds.

"Do you know Smokey?" Noelle inquired.

"Yeah." The brunette nodded, keeping her heated gaze on the security guard. "That man's trouble. I suggest you walk away."

"I hear you, but I need the money he's offering for information." Noelle grabbed the bottle by the neck, finishing the rest of the Corona. "I just don't know how to get to him."

"Your best bet are the guys over there." She nodded toward the men playing pool. "They are all connected to him in some way."

She didn't explain further.

Noelle eyed her new targets remembering one of Mia's tales about her friend, Cameron Stone, using a pool game to get close to Daron's team. "Are you up for a game?"

"Girl," she cackled. "I don't know how to play. It's the only way I knew to approach dude." She pulled out her cell, clicked a few keys. "I'll bet you a round of beers that they'll shut you down."

"I'll have to pass on that." She had taken in enough of their game to know she couldn't play since there were wagers involved. Noelle couldn't say she was trying to trade information for cash, then drop big money on a pool game. "But I'm still going for it."

The brunette stood. "You're crazy, lady."

Noelle tugged the bottom of her black sweatshirt over the gun tucked in her waistband and followed the stocky woman.

"Good luck." She winked at the security guard before changing direction and moving toward the restroom.

Noelle glanced at the men who had yet to acknowledge her presence. "Who's up for a friendly game of pool?"

"No one," the security guard snapped. "Now go away."

"That's cool. No one has the balls or the skills to play a woman?" Noelle took a few steps putting distance between herself and their table to make sure she caught their attention.

"Sorry," he shot back. "This section is restricted to VIP."

"That's fine." She walked away, then paused, glanced over her shoulder and said, "I didn't really want to play. I mistakenly thought a VIP wanted information on a florist."

Noelle reclaimed her stool at the same moment Zane entered the establishment. She followed his progression, taking in the broad shoulders and well-shaped rear end as he strode across the black-tiled floor, heading to a back booth. Zane peeled off his coat, showcasing his arm tats and she had to tear her eyes away from him. *Now that's a present I wouldn't mind unwrapping for the holidays.* Something about the entire package drew her attention, which was the precise reason she avoided him. She shook off her naughty thoughts as she remembered she was working.

"Jingle bells, you all right over there?"

Noelle nodded, noticing the bartender staring. She ordered another beer, hoping this night wasn't a bust. A man with light complexion moved away from the rowdy group, advancing toward the bar with a sexy swagger.

"Hello, Beautiful." He rested his lower back on the bar and gave her a seductive grin.

"Hola, Mr. I-didn't-introduce-myself." Noelle sipped her beer and gave a wink over the rim of her glass.

He leaned in, extending a hand. "Smokey. I hear you're looking for me."

Noelle played along, not convinced that the man she was talking to was the person he pretended to be. She leaned in and whispered, "How much you payin' for info?"

"A hundred. If it's information I haven't heard, it's a stack. Just know people who recycle information we already have don't fare well." He turned to face the bar, flashing his Sig Sauer P320 as he pulled out some cash and retrieved a hundred-dollar bill. "So talk."

Two men stood at tables close to them, causing the current occupants to relocate. Noelle realized she was really speaking to Smokey and not one of his lackeys.

"Elle, remember don't say too much," Zane reminded her seconds before the waitress approached him.

Noelle slid the hundred in front of her and repeated the same information Lloyd had given her and Zane.

Smokey moved until they were inches apart, peeling off more bills and laying them on the bar next to her. "I'd say be careful with all that cash, but my man tells me you're strapped." He stood and sauntered toward his friends without giving a backward glance.

The fact he gave Noelle a grand scared the hell out of her. *Did she just give them information to help track down Violet?* Noelle feared she'd provided them a key piece of information and would find Violet before they could. She had to figure out what that tidbit was and quickly.

Noelle didn't have time to fully digest that thought before Orlando, Rafael's former procurement manager, entered and walked over to the pool table section. Orlando was probably there doing what he did best, networking and making deals happen but she couldn't afford for him to see her. The moment his back was to her, she bolted like the devil was chasing her.

CHAPTER 6

The day had been draining and frustrating as Noelle spent most of it searching any video footage they could get along I-94 W in the direction the florist had been heading. She crossed off another one of the potential locations as she hung up, disconnecting from another person stating he hadn't seen anyone matching Violet's description. Occasionally her mind drifted to Orlando. *Had he seen her? Would he seek her out? Has he been visiting Rafael in prison? Is he the one looking to get the crew back together?*

Noelle shook off those questions. The bright spot in her day was another secret Santa gift. Mia's prime suspect was Zane. He was hers too until today's gift. Only a few people knew of her obsession with drawing and art. Zane wasn't one of them, so how would he know to gift her with an assortment of paints, chalks, and drawing pencils, along with several drawing pads? Not even her mother knew.

She shot off a text to check on her mother, knowing it was her least favorite time of the year. Noelle let her head rest on the headboard of the king-size bed in the master bedroom for a moment before going back to reviewing videos. Whenever her cousin was away from their temporary office, she worked from the bed as if she were at home. Her cell phone rang, and she glanced at the screen.

Noelle chuckled. "What's up, Mia?" She stood, heading to the desk, feeling like a kid caught doing something naughty.

"Are you with Zane?"

"Yes, and no." Her gaze immediately went to the door leading to the hallway. "Why you ask?"

"You were both logged in after hours. I thought you might have had a late-night *working* session," Mia said, in a teasing way. "And I could tell you both at the same time."

Until ten minutes ago, Zane had been working from her desk. He went down to the lobby to grab their dinner. "I'll update him when we're off the line."

Mia called out to Calvin that she'd be there in a minute, then said, "Violet emailed Kathy to approve the reception arrangements."

"Wait, what?"

Noelle listened as her cousin explained the florist sent a time delayed message to the wedding coordinator. It didn't go out when it should have, which was the day after she disappeared because her email server had a glitch. It delivered the message an hour ago.

"It's in your inbox. Dig a little further. Hold on." Mia yelled to Calvin that she was heading in now. "Got to go. We're about to receive a satellite call from Daron with updates about our trapped King."

"Let me—"

Mia ended the call and Noelle threw up her hands.

Daron and Nicco, a member of the Crossroads elite team, were in Durabia. Their next stop would be Ajid. Once they contacted the missing King, they'd have less than a day or two to adjust their plan to accommodate any new intel. If the situation required immediate extraction, the security team out of Durabia would handle it. Daron wanted the devices Calvin tweaked to minimize risk to his employees. Her fingers were crossed that the Chicago team would have enough time to fly in for the rescue and that she'd finish this assignment in time to be one of them.

"Holly. What has you staring out into space?" Zane asked, carrying a plastic bag.

The smell of the food made her stomach growl. She hopped from the chair, making tracks to the mini refrigerator. "I'm wondering if the Chicago team will do the extraction."

"Did you hear something?" Zane, with one hand, pulled the table where they kept snacks during meetings away from the wall, before setting the bag on it.

Noelle grabbed Zane's favorite sparkling water and a cola for herself. "Not about that. Mia and the crew are probably talking to Daron and getting an update as we speak." She placed the drinks on the side as he pulled two chairs to the table, then gave him the update on the florist.

"I'll have to check with our people to see if there's any way to track if she logs into her email." Zane retrieved his phone from the front pocket of his shirt and shot off the text before placing the device on the table. "Do you want me to bring your laptop?"

She admired his broad shoulders, tapered waist, and round behind that made her feel like she needed to add more squats to her workout routine. Noelle wondered if he had tattoos on his chest and back, a continuation of the amazing artwork on his arms.

"Holly." He stared down at the laptop.

"What do you think?" She turned to avoid eye contact, knowing Zane caught her gawking, and took the containers of food out of the bag.

Zane slid the computer next to her, then rounded the table and sat his laptop down. "I can't believe you can keep your figure eating all this." His hand swept over a feast that could feed an entire team.

"I did good. I also wanted shrimp tempura, vegetable pot stickers, spring rolls, and chicken teriyaki." Noelle had a hard time narrowing down her choices, since the restaurant they ordered from had Chinese, Thai, and Japanese menu items. She had a strategy for her order: egg roll, crab rangoon, fried rice, and orange beef for dinner. Shrimp toast was her late-night snack, and egg foo young would be breakfast.

"And don't think that means your sushi, cucumber salad, and salmon bowl are safe." She laughed as he playfully tugged his containers closer to him.

"Do you want me to take on the email angle?" He typed on the keyboard, she assumed to log into his laptop.

Noelle grabbed a crab rangoon and plopped it into her mouth. "I'll look at it. I need a break from the footage."

"Copy that." He picked up a few napkins and pushed the rest in her direction. "Any plans besides the wedding for the holidays?"

"Not really." Noelle was scheduled to be part of the wedding's security team. "Because of my childhood, it's really not my thing. But I do enjoy seeing friends and family I don't always get to catch up with through the year. Mia invited me to dinner, but I'm going to pass."

"My family is unique. My parents adopted me and my siblings, so we celebrate a multi-cultural Christmas." He explained that one brother was white, the others were Russian, East Indian, and Native American. He also had a Puerto Rican sister and a second sister, who like his parents, were African American.

Noelle found that tidbit fascinating. "What's that like?"

Before he could answer, the wedding coordinator's number appeared on her phone. She held up an index finger to quiet Zane as she answered Kathy's call.

"Noelle, I've copied you on the finalized arrangements, but I'm still concerned about the timing. Have you found her or another vendor?"

Zane stepped out of the room, with the laptop in one hand and phone in the other.

"We have a lead." Noelle didn't want to mention that the lotuses they found were not white. American lotuses were rarely white. White lotus that grew in the States were usually brought in from another region and planted in wetlands here.

"I know it's important to find her." Her voice broke as if the stress of the events had crept in. "But I need to know if I have to start working on the less than spectacular back-up plan."

Noelle glanced at Zane, who stopped pacing outside the door. His eyes held a glimmer of excitement. She was curious about what had happened. "Let me follow up with Harris, now that he has your selection, and find out what challenges we'll face in making it happen."

"Thank you."

"De nada. You're welcome," Noelle said, remembering to repeat the phrase in English. She ended the call and retrieved the email correspondence from the coordinator and Harris as Zane rushed in.

"We've got something." He lowered the laptop, sat it next to hers, and hit play.

She watched the footage, feeling a spark of hope. They finally had a solid lead on Violet. Evidently Lloyd wasn't the only one heading to Gurnee the night Violet disappeared.

CHAPTER 7

"That was definitely her car."

As they entered a men's store in the shopping mall, Zane glanced at Noelle, who was studying the still images of the video from the gas station on her phone. Chad, the person who had worked the day Violet purchased gas, wasn't in, but the footage was helpful. They planned to go back to speak to Chad when his shift started later.

Today Zane was knocking out two tasks with one swing. He verified that Violet's car had been spotted in Gurnee and she'd seemed to be heading from Illinois to Wisconsin, while picking up holiday gifts for the family. He hadn't expected Noelle to join him, but enjoyed the company, especially once he got her to stop talking shop. He returned his attention to looking for gifts for his brothers.

"Is this a corset for men?" Noelle picked up the red and silver vest.

He plucked it from her, staring at the string interlaced down the back. "Damn, I guess so."

"And it would look fabulous on you." The honey-blonde saleswoman sized him up with her eyes and showed him a black, blue, and silver vest, matching silver shirt and a blue tie. "You should try it on."

Zane moved to the sweater rack. "I'm shopping for my brothers, not myself."

She circled the table, landing on the side nearest him. "These three items can jazz up your black suit for any upcoming event."

"Try them on." Noelle gave him a mischievous grin. "I'm curious to see what the vest looks like on you."

He grabbed a couple sweaters one of his brothers would like and moved toward the register. "I don't even know how to get in that contraption."

"Come on, live a little." Noelle took the items from the woman and grinned. "Indulge me and try it on. Por favor." She held the vest out to him. "Please."

"Fine." He grimaced, taking the items from her. Noelle rarely said please in English or Spanish, so to hear her say it to him tugged at his heart string. "Where's the dressing room?" Zane followed the sales lady and quickly changed into the items. He stepped out a few moments later, and the saleswoman tugged on the strings at the base and he could feel the vest tightening around his waist.

"Go show your girlfriend how sexy you'll be looking for the holidays." She smiled, holding the curtain back so Noelle could see him.

Noelle's mouth dropped open, and she fumbled with the phone. "Well damn, that right there looks like fiyah on you." She smiled while snapping a picture. "Mr. Sexy, turn around so I can get one of the back of the vest. Caliente and muy elegante."

On Noelle's reaction only, Zane wanted to purchase the vest, loving that she thought it suited him.

Her eyes grew sad as she said, "You should get that for Dro's wedding."

Zane could only guess that she had been gut punched after

thinking that while they were out enjoying shopping, a businessman and Violet were missing and Dro was stuck in Ajid and wouldn't make his wedding if they didn't get him out soon. "I was on the losing end of the battle to be in that final count." He returned to the dressing room, changing into street clothes, and left the store with only a couple sweaters.

Two hours later, they headed to the vehicle with shopping bags and pretzel bites and other snacks for the ride home after their visit with Chad.

"It seems the weather changed a little bit while we were inside." Noelle's steps slowed as they reached the door and saw it was now covered in a blanket of snow.

"Yes." Zane whipped out his phone to check the weather. "When I asked Roc permission to mix business with pleasure, the weather report said flurries in Chicago, a couple of inches in the southern suburbs, and Indiana would get the heaviest snowfall. This area looked good."

Noelle glanced down at his phone. "How bad is it?"

"Not bad. It looks like what has fallen is it. These flurries supposed to clear up in an hour." He shifted the bags to one hand and retrieved his keys.

"We'll see." She zipped up her coat, looking doubtful.

The cold air and snow blasted Zane as they walked to the SUV. He threw the bags in the trunk and made quick work of cleaning the vehicle off as Noelle rushed into the passenger side.

"What's the game plan?" Noelle turned up the heat, looking at him as if she was hoping he'd changed his mind about hitting a few stores in an outside mall in Kenosha, WI.

"Let's go talk to Chad, then head home." Zane slowly made his way out of the parking lot, hoping the street condition was better.

Noelle glanced at her watch. "He doesn't start for another thirty minutes."

"Yeah, but we need to park out of camera view again and walk to the gas station." Zane was grateful that it was connected to a fast food restaurant for them to kill some time and stay warm.

Fifteen minutes later, Noelle sat across from him staring into the gas station.

"What was your favorite holiday tradition as a kid?" Zane asked, then sipped a large sweet tea.

"My mom wasn't really into Christmas." Noelle played with the crispy fries as if lost in her memories. "Her lack of enthusiasm around Christmas is what made me curious about Kwanzaa."

"Interesting." He kept his expression neutral although that fact surprised him. "Christmas is really about the traditions you create with those you love. I emerged in a world with unusual family traditions, but growing up that way, I've learned to respect various cultures and tried to be sensitive to their plight. So when I say Happy Holidays instead of Merry Christmas, which is what I celebrate, it's me being respective of people's differences."

Zane's soul stirred as he realized they were connecting on a deeper level than physical attraction. Noelle placed a hand over his, which pulled his focus from the convenience store area of the gas station and onto her soulful eyes.

"Did you feel disconnected?" he asked, studying her golden-brown skin.

Noelle nodded. "My father's from Mexico. I want to learn the culture I missed out on." She spun his phone around on the table with an index finger. "What my life would have been if I'd known that side of my family."

"I don't know my full history but I never let that prevent me from appreciating the blessing in the family that I do have." He glanced at his watch. Chad was late. Hopefully, it wasn't anything to be concerned about.

"Have you taken an ancestry test?"

"No. Knowing that information won't change the fact that I wasn't raised by my birth parents and didn't experience their traditions, rituals, or get to know their family history." He felt the edge of his lips curl up as Noelle's fingers caressed his.

Noelle withdrew her hand and swept a braid behind an ear. "Will you eventually?"

"I probably will when I find the right woman and we decide to forge a life together." Zane stared at her lips as she leaned forward and gazed up at him. As desire sparked in her eyes, he hoped he'd already found his soul mate.

He closed the gap as she shifted closer to him. A scream pierced the air and Noelle jumped back seconds before their lips touched. Zane hopped up to see Chad being yanked backwards toward the door. Noelle tossed him the phone from the table as they raced over. It vibrated in his hand as he slid it in a coat pocket.

"Dude, there's nothing else I can tell you." Chad held on to the doorjamb to stop his assailant's movement.

"Like I said," the tall, muscular man reached for him again. "I have more questions."

"Gentlemen is there a problem?" Zane asked pushing through the small crowd gathering in the aisle.

"This ain't none of your business." The man released Chad and swung at Zane.

Zane ducked the punch then issued an uppercut to his chin. Noelle moved Chad to safety and kept the people back, spreading both arms. A kick to the man's abdomen sent him crashing into a stand of chips. The stranger shot forward tackled Zane in the abs, propelling both to the floor. Zane slammed his elbow to the back of the attacker when another man entered with an AK-47.

"The fight is over," the masked man yelled.

People scattered as Zane released his hold then put up his hands, noticing Noelle had a weapon pointed at the gunman. The assailant scrambled to his feet and when he passed his partner, the man backed away and said, "We got what we need."

Once the gunman cleared the threshold, Zane rushed to the

door to see the same sedan from Paige's house pulling out of the lot.

"You okay?" Noelle asked, glancing at Chad, who remained near the counter talking to a co-worker.

Zane nodded and retrieved his phone to send Roc a text. He could hear sirens in the distance getting closer.

"Chad knows nothing more than that Violet headed back towards the expressway."

Zane had forgotten he'd received a text as the incident occurred. Reading Roc's text, he realized this trip turned out to be a blessing in more ways than one. First one being, Zane felt for the first time that he had really bonded with Noelle. Second, they were in position to handle what was coming.

"Roc got a lead on Violet." Zane shook his head when excitement flashed in her brown eyes. "He's tracking Smokey and his men, and they're heading our way to silence her permanently."

CHAPTER 8

"Do you know why they kidnapped the Chamberlain?"

Noelle peered out of the window at the road that had been cleared of snow, then glanced down at the tracker. They had gotten on the expressway when the GPS said that the vehicles were passing the exit where they had been waiting. Now the two SUVs they'd been trailing had gone in different directions. Zane followed the man in the Land Rover who called himself Smokey, and Roc's team took the Chevrolet Tahoe.

"The only thing that made sense was the rumor he was attempting to purchase an abandoned building to create a community center."

"I take it Smokey's using it to run his illegal business." Noelle pulled out her phone to do an internet search.

"I'm not sure." Zane shifted the angle of the phone holder. "We're coming up empty on connecting it to Smokey."

She shook her head as a truck flew past at high speed, as if the road wasn't slick. "I don't want to sound cruel, but why not kill him?"

"After some digging, I'm guessing it's about making him miss a deadline. He has to sign the contract by Christmas, or the building goes back on the market."

"Smokey needs Violet gone because she probably messes up the narrative they were trying to spin on the abduction." Noelle pushed down on an imaginary brake as a car slid in front of them with barely enough room to avoid an accident.

The file Roc had sent over suggested several deals had fallen through. Based on the history of the building, she wondered if Smokey used these same tactics to continue using it for free. Noelle had many questions about what kind of business he was running out of there.

"Maybe the plan was to make it seem he left on his own to indulge in some dirty deals." Zane passed the Land Rover and glided in front of an eighteen-wheeler. He occasionally made that maneuver when they were a suitable distance between exit ramps. A risky move, but their targets were less likely to think they were being followed. The only thing she hated was they were in Zane's personal vehicle, a Porsche Cayenne GTS, and not one of the company vehicles that would lead back to Crossroads Security instead of his home. Yes, he had parked a block away and walked to the gas station but now they were tracking dangerous people. "Why do you think that's the play?"

"Haven't you noticed all the tips now coming out in the media about seeing Chamberlain getting in a car of his own accord or spotting him with some dark-haired lady?"

She had, but wrote it off as people attempting to get their thirty seconds of airtime. "Why the sudden smear campaign? Why not start that when the investigation first began? Are they trying to stop the police from looking into it? Lo siento. You don't have these answers any more than I do." Noelle paused, realizing she'd said I'm sorry in Spanish. "Lo siento means…"

"I know what it means." Zane's lips lifted in that irritating know-it-all smirk. "I'm fluent in several languages."

That shouldn't have surprised her, but it did. Not only that, but it was also a slight turn on. She reached into the backseat, grabbing her purse to check what kind of weaponry she had on her. Plus, she needed to focus on something other than the fact that every day she spent with Zane her attraction to him grew at an alarming rate. Not to mention she almost kissed him in a public place while working.

She had a couple of inconspicuous weapons and a Ruger LC9S in the bag, but didn't have any backup ammo.

Zane allowed Smokey's Land Rover to pass him, along with two other cars, before sliding back into the slow lane. The SUV took the next off ramp and stayed on the side streets until they turned off on a gravel path.

Noelle grabbed his phone to examine the map of the area. "They're turning but the road isn't showing on the map. It must be a private road or a driveway."

Zane rode past the gravel path and turned off on the next street. Smokey and his driver would have spotted them if they followed. They drove through the quiet residential area. The further they went, the more distance opened up between the houses.

He glanced at her. "Have they stopped moving?"

"Not yet." Noelle looked at the street name, which seemed familiar. From her phone, she retrieved the list of potential locations where the florist could be hiding. "But I'm pretty sure they know where she is."

"Why do you say that?"

"This is the block where Violet's second summer home is located." Noelle wondered how they found it since it wasn't under her married or maiden name. A cousin bought it for her but left it in his name. He did the upkeep and handled the rental but made her a beneficiary if anything happened to him.

"Let's go there first." Zane picked up speed, clearly racing to an address he seemed to know by heart.

They stopped in front of a large house, mint-green siding, and stone accents on the base of the structure. Several thin trees were scattered across the lawn and low bushes dotted the front yard. Larger shrubs lined the back half of the driveway providing ample cover.

"I don't see her car." She scanned the area, then pulled out mascara and lipstick.

Zane frowned and his nose wrinkled as if he smelled something bad. "You're not about to get made-up, are you?"

She shook her head and pushed the button to release the blade hidden in the mascara, then retracted it. "Trust me when I say you don't want this …" She held up the lipstick. "…On your skin." Noelle slid the two items into her jacket pocket.

Zane updated the team, then exited the Porsche, pulling out a Smith & Wesson M&P. "I'll check around back."

"I'll ring the doorbell. So keep an eye out for any movement." She slid the Ruger into her waistband and glanced in both directions.

The single streetlight flickered on as she waited for Zane to advance up the driveway before she walked the salted pavement to the stairs and onto a large, covered porch. She pressed the doorbell, then moved to the window to look for any movement.

After a few minutes, Zane returned and rested a foot on the bottom step and leaned on the white hand railing. "I don't think she's here."

She met him at the bottom, and they headed back to the Porsche. "I agree." Noelle hadn't seen any lights go off, heard any footsteps in the house, and not a single curtain shifted. If the property had a security system, it was well hidden.

He pulled off and backed the SUV against a barn-like structure sitting across the street from the house. "Why don't you wait here for her?" Zane grabbed the phone with the tracking app. "I'm going to check out what they're up to and what we are up against."

"Be safe." Noelle took his place behind the wheel. "I'll let you know when she shows up."

"Text me, *No Elle*." He held up the phone as if to remind her they didn't have their usual means of communication.

"Gotcha." She smiled slightly, recognizing this was as close as he had gotten to calling her by her actual name. Broken up into two words, but at least it was closer than Jingle Bells, Nelly, or Holly.

Zane cut through the trees, and she watched, concerned about the footprints he was leaving in the snow. She wished they had time to link up with Roc and grab some equipment before following them, but he sent the tracking link to Zane's phone.

Twenty minutes later, Violet showed up, turned into the drive-way, and parked in what looked like a storage shed in the back yard. The woman cautiously scanned the area as if she could feel someone watching before she entered the house. Noelle hopped out of the vehicle. Walking to the door was best since she didn't want to alert the florist and cause her to run while Noelle was parking in front of the house.

She pressed the doorbell. "Violet, I'm Noelle with Crossroads Security. If you reach out to your daughter, you'll see that we're here to help."

After five minutes of silence, she was about to head back to the car. Inside the house, the phone rang twice, and Noelle assumed Violet was answering it. Noelle paused, pulled out her phone, and realized she hadn't texted Zane.

She'd barely hit send when the white lace curtains shifted and few seconds later, the door opened. The florist yanked her inside and closed the door. She put an index finger to her lips.

What a hell of a welcome.

Noelle didn't have to contemplate long on Violet's action. Cars were rapidly coming up the street.

"Sorry to pull you into this," Violet whispered.

Noelle whipped out her Ruger, moved the florist away from the door, and peeked out the window. Three vehicles rolled onto the snowy lawn and six men stepped out.

"This is your last chance to accept the offer, or your ashes will become lawn fertilizer," a male voice called out.

When one of the men pulled a machine gun from the trunk, Noelle prayed Zane was on his way back. Things were about to get heated.

CHAPTER 9

Zane hated that he hadn't grabbed surveillance equipment and extra weapons since shopping for gifts for his family and should have only been doing routine interviews. He had to figure out how to approach the log cabin without notifying the occupants. A slightly cracked window drew his attention. He raced down the slippery stairs to avoid leaving snowy prints and aimed for the spot between the two glass panes. The pungent smell of Cuban cigars seeped into the air as he listened in and watched the two men inside.

"It's in place," a Latino man said to Smokey. "We have it set to go off within the hour. If she doesn't return in the next thirty minutes, we'll go in and adjust the timer."

A third guy with silver hair entered the room, laughing. He appeared older than the others but Zane couldn't see his face. "Too bad I can't watch her facial expression when she realizes it's a trap. Whether she stays or goes, she dies. Unless she agrees, but we all know she won't."

Zane pondered what Violet could agree to that could save her life. He texted Roc the florist's address along with a brief update.

Roc responded *we're on the way*.

Smokey retrieved a Maxim 9 from the kitchen table and glanced at the taller man. "Pack up while I take a leak."

"Don't want to be caught with your zipper down again?" The older man laughed, taking a puff of his cigar that had been laying in an ashtray on the table near the electronics.

Smokey's retreating footsteps stopped. "Funny, I believe it was you, old man, who got caught slipping hence why I'm here," he shot back. "Maybe if you'd let me use my own team, I'd get better results."

Zane's phone vibrated in his pocket as the other guy called out, "The eagle has landed."

He slid the cell out and glanced at the message from Noelle, confirming the same information on Violet's return home.

"Get them in position. Tell them to make the last offer, but don't make a move unless she tries to escape." The older man looked down at the expensive timepiece on his wrist. "When he's done taking care of business, head that way. Don't screw things up like y'all did last time."

Zane wondered who was the older man as he eased away from the cabin, careful not to make a sound. He crept back up the trail he came from, even though he couldn't follow his track because he'd wiped them away with a fallen tree branch. The prints left were near the Porsche, and the route he'd taken didn't make them easily visible from the road. He didn't have time to care about footprints on the return trip as he hustled through trees and snow.

When he was far enough from the cabin, he pulled out the phone and hands-free device, then used the voice command to call Noelle. "You and Violet need to get out now."

"We're trying to." Noelle informed him of what had happened. They were attempting to get out the side door that was closer to the rear of the house to reach the florist's vehicle.

"Don't wait for me, get as far away as you can." He adjusted the earpiece, picking up speed. "I'll meet up with you later."

"How? I have your keys."

His heart muscle tightened at the concern in her voice, but he was more worried about them. Even if he made it before they left, Smokey's people would outnumber them at least until Roc and the team arrived. "Roc is heading this way."

Zane ended the call, the dimming sunlight made it challenging to spot his markers. He felt as though he'd never make it to the destination until the Porsche finally came into view. He took one look at the driveway and realized Noelle and Violet had not made it out. Two men kneeled at the front of the house, boarding up the window at the base of the building. Another man crept out the side door, picked up wood laying nearby, nodded at the approaching fellow with more material tucked under his arms, then headed around the back. Zane assumed there were more men on the other side of the house.

The man never heard or saw Zane coming behind him. One blow had him falling to the salty ground. The second blow knocked him unconscious. Zane dragged him across the driveway and into the bushes, then rushed toward the entrance. He was about to crash his elbow through the glass pane when he remembered the man coming out the door. He twisted the knob instead. The door opened without issue. Zane crept up the stairs looking for Noelle and came face to face with a Ruger.

She quickly lowered the weapon. "I almost shot you."

"Ladies, we need to move before they realize they're a man down." He held an index finger up after hearing a bump.

"That's probably the furnace," Violet whispered as she peered from behind Noelle.

He opened the nearby door, and the florist gasped. The noise wasn't the furnace; it was the missing businessman. His mouth gagged and hands cuffed to a pole in the utility room.

"Help him, please. He saved my life." Violet surged forward and snatched the gag.

Both Zane and Noelle's heads snapped in her direction, waiting for further explanation but one didn't come. They had the story all wrong. The florist was the target, and Chamberlain had been the unfortunate witness.

"You don't carry handcuff keys, do you?" Chamberlain slid the metal over the pipe.

Violet stepped back as Zane moved closer, examining the cuffs, while trying to decide the best way to get them off.

He glanced over a shoulder, hoping the florist had a pin on her that he could use to pick the lock. She was gone and Noelle was studying an object on the furnace. Banging in the distance could only mean the men were back to boarding up the window and the door in the back to force Violet out into the firing squad.

"Tell me this is not a bomb." Noelle pointed at the items attached to the furnace.

Zane examined the device and grimaced. "We have twenty minutes to get out of here." Zane thought back to the man's comment about adjusting the timer. Based on the countdown, the florist had come home before the reset.

"Please don't leave me." The man tugged at the cuffs. "I don't want to die because I tried to help her."

"I'm sorry. I got this." She pushed Zane back, took out the lipstick and rubbed the mauve wax on the center of the cuff. The lipstick bubbled, melting the metal.

"I'll find Violet, so we'll be ready to get out of here." Zane glanced at the time, knowing they needed every minute. They had to figure out how to exit the house without getting shot.

"I'm here." She appeared in the doorway with a book bag on her back and a coat in hand. "I went to see if we could make it to the shed out back. But they boarded up the side door and the back windows, too ... as well as get something for him ..." She nodded toward Chamberlain, who was only wearing an open shirt, slacks, and shoes.

Zane set the timer on his watch, shaving off a two-minute cushion. He trotted down the stairs while Noelle applied more lipstick to the cuffs. Examining the boards on the back window, he debated if he could break them.

If they planted the bomb, they would have taken anything Violet could have used to break down the thick wood over the windows and doors. They were counting on her not to jump out of a window on the upper level.

Zane's current solution was shooting their way out. The odds were, someone on both sides wouldn't make it out alive.

CHAPTER 10

Zane wondered if there were more explosives hidden around the house. He returned to the group. "Let's move. We need to figure a way out before the house explodes and without getting ourselves gunned down."

The ladies didn't need him to say any more. They raced up the stairs toward their best chance of escape. Chamberlain, in his new winter coat, swayed a bit, probably dealing with whatever drugs were in his system. He almost tripped over the rug as they entered the living room.

After lifting the curtains, Zane's pulse raced when he saw three vehicles facing the house with two men standing on either side of each car with their weapons drawn. The man he had knocked out somehow recovered quickly.

"What's the plan?" Noelle peeked through the window and her eyes widened, but she quickly reigned in her reaction when she realized Violet and Chamberlain were staring at her. "I guess negotiations are over."

With the last of the daylight fading, they had a fighting chance. "Call Roc and see if he's close enough to lend us a hand."

Smokey's team had set the trap well, giving them only a couple of thin trees to provide cover. The chances of making it to a tree from the front door were slim. Zane studied their enemy's position, fanned out on the lawn. The only way of getting by them was on the side, which is why they boarded up the rear side door. Getting a weakened man and the petite florist out of the upper window without injuries would be a challenge. If Roc was still too far off, it was a risk they'd have to take. Better injured than being dead.

Noelle walked over to him and whispered, "They're seven minutes away."

That would cut it too close. The team had five minutes tops to shut Smokey's team down and get everyone inside out of the house and to safety. "Look for something, anything, we can use to draw their attention away from the front door."

Noelle nodded and dashed across the room.

Zane rushed around the side of the house and realized they probably had an out. "Violet are there stairs by this window?"

"Yes." Violet's eyes lit up as though she understood his idea. "We sealed up the door and put a window in. Instead of ripping out the stairs, we hid them with bushes."

He lifted the window and brushed away the snow, knowing he had to send the weakest link out first. Zane knelt in front of the man who had taken a seat on the couch. "Are you well enough to run?"

"My legs are a little shaky, but I can manage." Chamberlain pressed down on the arm of the couch to stand.

"Noelle, we have an exit strategy." Zane explained the plan, then said, "Toss me the truck keys." He caught the keys Noelle threw, stepped through the window and used a boot to make a clearing on the landing. Zane hit the button once to unlock the truck, looking for the glow of the interior light to confirm the driver's door was open. He turned to assist Chamberlain through the window. "You see that light glow in the distance?" He pointed to the vehicle tucked near the back corner of the barn across the way. "That's where you're headed."

"Okay." Chamberlain gripped the rail tightly as he went down the slippery stairs.

"When you hear gunfire, run." Zane helped the florist onto the outside landing. "Once in the driver's seat, unlock the doors from the inside and don't start the car unless those men come toward you."

"This way," Zane directed, handing Violet the Porsche keys when they reached the bottom of the stairs. "Both of you wait there." He pointed to the bush at the corner of the house. "Remember, let him go first. When he's clear, go as quickly and quietly as possible."

Noelle focused on him as he raced back up the steps. "You think this is going to work?"

"It's our only shot." He climbed through the opening back into the house.

Zane opened the front window and fired two shots that took out the middle car's headlights. Noelle, who was at the window on the other side, shattered the light of the car nearest their escape route. Taking would allow them a better shot of the men and help hide their escape. The gunfire pounded the house. Neither of them had enough bullets to keep the gun fight going for long. Zane army crawled across the floor, reaching the area Noelle had just abandoned as the bullets slowed. He fired several more shots from there hitting two of the men as Noelle went out the escape window.

"They both are in the vehicle," Noelle confirmed as she slid next to him.

"Okay." Zane blew out a sigh of relief. He peeked out to see the men advancing toward the door. He tried to get Noelle to make her escape before him, but she refused to leave without him. "We need to fire these last shots, then move."

Once they returned fire and took out the last car lights, Noelle headed out the window. Zane shot out the streetlight before leaving. The bullets were still hitting the house as he stepped onto the landing.

Noelle had already made it to the bush at the corner of the house. She glanced back, and he waved her on and raced down the stairs and onto the driveway.

She peered around the corner, then dashed off. Before Zane made it to the front, a man darted out, grabbed Noelle and thew her to the ground. They wrestled in the driveway with whipping wind and gun fire as their soundtrack. Zane aimed, but couldn't get a clear shot.

"They're getting away," the man called out.

Zane's watch beeped, alerting him he only had a minute to clear the blast as he raced toward her.

She pulled out the mascara, released the blade, and stabbed the assailant in the leg.

The man yelped.

Zane ripped the guy off Noelle, prepared to use him as a shield. He fired a round into the shooting arm of the nearest approaching man, knowing he had no more bullets. The man clutched his wounded arm then bolted as Noelle hopped to her feet. When Zane noticed the rest of the men were retreating to their cars, he shoved Noelle's attacker causing him to collapse to the ground. He hopped to his feet and ran off as if he wasn't injured.

Looking at the distance they'd covered, Zane realized they were too close to the house. He pivoted toward the SUV and yelled, "Run!"

They dashed across the driveway seconds before the explosion. The force knocked them to the ground. Zane shielded her body with his as the debris from the building flew around them. When he thought it was safe, he rolled off her.

"Gracias a Dios." Noelle lay on her back, breathing heavily. "I thought I was going to survive the explosion, only to die by suffocation."

Zane laughed, then stood, noticing that Roc and law enforcement had blocked the three cars in. "That's why you're thanking God?" He shook his head and extended a hand to help her up.

"Dude, you're no lightweight." She smiled, brushing some debris off his shoulder. "Try a plank move for the next protective shield." She rose on tiptoe and planted a kiss on his cheek. "All kidding aside, thanks."

Zane didn't get to savor the moment because another explosion rocked the house, forcing him to usher Noelle to the safety of the awaiting Porsche.

CHAPTER 11

"*K*wanzaa are you..." Noelle inhaled and swallowed the curse word that was on the tip of her tongue. "Are you kidding me?"

Mia grimaced. "There seems to have been a little miscommunication."

"What happened?" She glanced at Mia, packing the electronics into crates then at the two men breaking down the desks.

Mia pursed her lips like she was trying to keep her anger in check. "Before Violet went missing, the wedding was moved to Kwanzaa."

Noelle shot to her feet. "And Kathy's just *now* notifying us."

"A new employee assumed Kathy had already told us since we were in contact with her about the florist and left us off the memo. Only problem, in Kathy's mind the date change wasn't important enough to mention since it was only one day."

"Can I shoot her?" Noelle was fuming but proud of herself for not using every curse word she knew to express herself.

The edges of Mia's lips curled up slightly before she issued a stern look. "Lola and Dro's wedding has enough challenges without you murdering their coordinator."

"You're right, but I'm still pissed about it."

Mia chuckled. "Wasn't asking you not to be."

"I could've had this done if I'd known the wedding is on Kwanzaa. Some florists wouldn't work on Christmas and the rest were booked. That one day would have made a huge difference." Noelle wanted to sue the woman for unnecessary stress. "I have no words. Kathy better be glad Violet needed help." She shook her head in frustration.

"Is that why we're packing up?" Noelle shifted out of the doorway to allow one of the men to roll the cart with her workstation into the hallway. Her plan to double check that she didn't leave Shanay's gift in one of the desk drawers was up in smoke.

"No. The decision was made that it was best for everyone to work out of the main office." Mia secured the lid on the final crate and nodded for the guy to take it away. "Look on the bright side, your main focus can return to bringing Dro home for his wedding."

Noelle understood that getting the groom back for the wedding was always the team's top priority. "Good point."

"After what happened with the Violet rescue, I realized we need to get you out of the office more often to keep your security training fresh," Mia explained, scanning the room as though checking for anything she'd missed.

"Not too much." Noelle forced a smile on her face. "I like what I do." She preferred helping remotely to avoid running into anyone from her former life.

"If you change your mind about coming through for dinner, text me." Mia slipped on her coat.

Noelle followed Mia to the door, checking her watch. She didn't want to miss her train to Downers Grove. "I'm meeting an old friend. If we part ways at a reasonable time, I'll roll through."

Mia raised a perfectly arched eyebrow.

"Not him. As far as I know he's still in prison," Noelle said, referring to her ex-boyfriend. When she didn't want her family to know who she was seeing, she always referred to Rafael that way.

Mia smiled but doubt flickered in her eyes. "FYI. You and Zane will continue to work together to find out the identity of the older man at the cabin."

"He's the real threat to the wedding if he goes after Violet again." As they made their way to the parking lot, Noelle hoped he wasn't connected to her past. "This could be the quiet before the storm."

Mia gave her a quick hug before they parted ways. "Good job with the florist."

"Gracias." Noelle laughed when she remembered where she left the gift — in the car's trunk in a tote bag with her mother's presents.

She grabbed it, hustled to the train station, and made it with minutes to spare. Noelle didn't want to think about work. It made her nervous that Mia wanted her to work the security side more during a time where she needed to lie low and stay off people's radar. Part of her wondered if Shanay had dabbled back into the old lifestyle. Shanay hadn't quite broken ties with their community as Noelle had. Despite that, Noelle still enjoyed their pre-holiday get together and gift exchange.

Lost in thought, Noelle almost missed the stop. She popped up when they announced Downers Grove, exited the train, and walked briskly to a cozy bar. The place was filled with customers as she searched the area looking for a familiar face. A tall, shapely woman wearing a designer jogging suit waved from the bar. Noelle squeezed through the sea of people until she reached her. She removed her coat and purse from the seat next to her.

"Noelle, I thought I'd have to fight someone to keep them from jacking this seat."

"I'm glad you didn't come to blows." Noelle sat the gift in front of Shanay. "This joint seems to get busier and busier every year."

They had met there ever since the year Rafael was arrested. Noelle still couldn't believe five years had passed from when everything went down. Thoughts of work faded into the background as Noelle shared drinks and laughs while Shanay updated her on the most recent tales from the streets. She was about to give Noelle the latest info on the hunt for Rafael's inner circle when someone tapped Shanay on the shoulder.

A deep voice slurred out the words. "Can I buy your next drink?"

Shanay turned to respond to the man and things went downhill. The sassiness faded from her eyes as they widened like a deer trapped in headlights. "Coco, run!" She grabbed her purse and jacket.

Shanay calling her by her nickname indicated big trouble headed their way. Noelle snatched her things, sprang from the barstool and raced through the thick crowd.

Shanay pushed past a red-haired man sipping a drink near the back exit.

"Watch it," he screamed as the dark ale sloshed out of the glass. His eyes grew bigger as he looked beyond Noelle.

Noelle didn't even want to know what he saw. She kept her focus on the blonde ponytail in front of her as Shanay did her best impression of a track star.

"Haul ass, Coco." She pushed through the crowd with Noelle on her heels.

"Nay-Nay don't run," one of the men yelled.

Looking back, Noelle saw four men racing after them. It wasn't until she caught a glimpse of Dom's tall and muscular frame exiting the bar's side door that she truly freaked out. *What the hell? Why was an enforcer chasing Shanay?*

A bullet pinged off the dumpster in the alley as Noelle rounded the corner into a parking lot. Shanay jumped into a white Tucson and swung the door open for Noelle.

Noelle's legs barely were in the car before the door slammed shut as Shanay pulled off like a NASCAR driver.

"What is going on?" Noelle asked as she braced herself. "Why are they chasing you? You're no longer about that life."

"You mean why are they chasing *us*?" Shanay gunned through the yellow light. "It seems Talon wants Rafael's inner circle, minus the one who got him sent to prison."

No one seemed to have followed them from the bar but Shanay sped through the streets like they were on a high speed chase. Minutes later, Shanay slowed the SUV to a normal speed.

"Damn. I'm not in Rafael's inner circle."

"Not officially. But that snake in the grass, Antwan, outed you as the global distribution mastermind. Hence why you were taken in for questioning." Shanay huffed. "I suspect Talon wants your skill the most."

When Shanay issued the warning, Noelle expected old acquaintances demanding their help, or info on Rafael's business. What she didn't anticipate was that person to be Dom "The Undertaker" Keller. His body count for those who said no to his boss was notorious.

CHAPTER 12

Over the last few days, floral delivery hijacking across the city increased, some even turned violent. At least two drivers had been shot and the Crossroads Security team had found one man who managed several warehouses dead. Zane was certain he knew who was behind it but the why he hadn't discovered yet.

The real mystery Zane wanted to figure out was why Noelle had become so hyperaware of her surroundings. Even when they were off the clock and hanging out, she was assessing their location in a way that made Zane wonder if she was in trouble.

One good thing that had developed was they were extremely close to executing the plan to rescue their people who were trapped in Ajid.

Zane picked up a work vehicle, then slid behind the wheel and called Roc. "I'm meeting Harris first before I join the team at the floral delivery truck."

"Alone?" Roc asked.

"It shouldn't be dangerous. I suspect Harris wants protection outside of work." He maneuvered the car onto the main street. "I don't know why he didn't ask over the phone."

"You and Noelle will be in the truck tonight," Roc paused. "See you in two."

Zane drove to Harris' house, frustrated that his thirty-minute trip had taken an hour. Now he'd be rushing to stay on time for the delivery assignment. He turned onto a street that reminded him of a country road with no sidewalk and ditches running near the edge of the road except at the driveway. Pulling up to the house, he noticed two cars parked side by side. A shot rang out.

He called 9-1-1. "A shot has been fired." Zane gave the address, ignoring the dispatch question as he approached the home and entered through the ajar front door. He disconnected the call, slid the phone into a pocket, retrieved a Smith & Wesson M&P and slowly advanced toward the first door. He found himself in a foyer with two doors on either side and a hallway in front of him. Voices came from further down the hall.

His Smith & Wesson led the way as he moved through the corridor. To the left was the stylish living room and to the right was the kitchen. Harris and another man were in chairs facing each other with the gunman in between them pointing the weapon at the guy Zane didn't recognize. From his angle, Zane couldn't tell if anyone else was in the living room. Based on the size of Harris's friend, no way the attacker could have taken down those two alone. Unless he threatened Harris to get the other guy to cooperate.

Zane needed to make a move soon, but without knowing how many others were in the room he could get them all killed.

He tried to line up a shot but couldn't make it without injuring Harris. *Why couldn't the shooter be taller?*

"I told you what I know, so please go," Harris whimpered.

The gunman looked at him and gave an evil snicker, then turned back to the bruised and bloody man.

Zane holstered his weapon, then reached into his cargo pants' pocket for a light bomb. It would disorient the people inside long enough for him to make a move. He rolled the small silver ball into the room.

"What the hell?" The gunman looked down at the device.

The lights flashed and the man covered his eyes, then kicked the device out of the way.

Zane charged inside noticing there was only one hostile in the room. "Can anyone join the party?" He asked seconds before he slammed the man into the fireplace. The weapon hit the mantel and clattered to the floor. Zane delivered a blow to the man's jaw.

The attacker slammed his fist into Zane's neck. Zane kneed him in the gut, flipped him and twisted an arm behind his back.

A shot rang out, hitting the wall next to them. "You have less than three seconds to release him or these two men die."

Zane let the guy go, lifted his hands, and glanced at the new man with the rifle. His mind ran through possible scenarios that didn't get him killed, but there wasn't one.

The guy scrambled to retrieve the gun from the floor, aiming the weapon at Zane. "Welcome to the party."

The newcomer backed into the kitchen and dragged out a chair. "Tie him up. Stop running your mouth and handle your business." He slid the chair across toward his partner and aimed it to the opposite side of where Zane stood.

While the weapon was lowered, Zane rushed for the chair, grabbed the back and hit the newcomer with it. Zane then kicked his partner in the gut as he fired off a shot that hit a wall in the kitchen. Zane wrestled over the rifle. He swung the assailant where his partner didn't have a shot without both of them in it.

The man released his hold on the gun, causing Zane to stumble backward.

"Watch out," Harris screamed as the second man picked up a lamp from the side table.

Zane pivoted, and the lamp hit him in the shoulder. He drove an elbow into one man's neck and a fist into the other's face.

Sirens in the distance must have caught the newcomer's attention because he delivered two jabs and an upper cut that left Zane slightly stunned. He followed by jamming the rifle into Zane's midsection which dropped him to his knees.

"Let's get out of here," he said, dashing down the hallway.

As the second man attempted to get past him, Zane grabbed his leg, causing him to fall in the hallway. Zane quickly restrained, then lifted him from the floor, and tied him to the chair. He untied Harris then his friend.

"I wasn't much protection," the injured man muttered.

"Get some towels." Zane assessed the man's wounds. He put pressure on the worst, which was a gunshot in his abdomen.

Harris rushed into the kitchen and grabbed some items. He returned, pushed Zane out the way, and then applied pressure. "You need to go. I told them where Violet's new warehouse is located."

CHAPTER 13

oelle's nerves were on edge after she thought she'd seen Orlando when Roc stopped at the gas station. It could have been that stop was where the last driver was attacked. Her body stilled as a dark Yukon pulled up alongside them. Looking over the driver, she didn't recognize him but the passenger, Dom "The Undertaker". Now she thought she should've followed Shanay lead and left town for a few weeks.

"Roc gun it," Noelle yelled as the Yukon swerved to make impact with the truck.

She braced herself against whatever she could as Roc weaved in and out of traffic like a mad man. Bullets pinged off the truck.

"They're trying to shoot out the tires." Roc took one hand off the steering wheel and unclipped his weapon's holster.

Noelle glanced back. "The follow car is blocked in."

"If they get too close, we're going to have to back them off." He tapped his firearm.

Noelle needed Roc to get away from Dom and not engage in a gun battle with him.

Roc's phone rang, and he answered then put it on speaker.

"Where are you?" Zane asked.

"Being chased by the hijackers in your place," Roc answered, swerving between two slow cars.

"It's a distraction, the real team is heading to the warehouse." Zane summarized the Harris incident.

Noelle hoped Dom wasn't calling in reinforcement. She didn't want to tell them she was the reason the delivery truck was being attacked. Yet she couldn't let them take on two gangs at once.

Roc took a hard left and continued making turns until they were heading back to the warehouse. The follow car took that as an opportunity to get in between the truck and the Yukon to slow them down.

Meanwhile, Roc coordinated more of the team to meet at the warehouse.

Upon arriving, Noelle was sent to the surveillance van with Linc while Roc and the team entered the building. She called Violet for the location of the items for the Reyes/Samuels wedding but got voice mail. Noelle asked via text, hoping for a quicker response. Ten minutes after Roc entered the building, the Yukon pulled up to the delivery truck.

"Roc, you have two more entering the building," Linc announced. "Law enforcement is about twenty minutes out."

Fifteen minutes later, a light rapping came on the van's side panel. The back door slid open, and Zane stepped in, smiling at Noelle. "What's going on?"

She waved as he closed the door. Noelle stared at the bright red spots on his face wondering if he'd have bruising, or whether it would fade.

"The team has been discreetly reducing the opposition." Linc handed Zane a communication device, which he slipped into his ear.

Noelle returned her focus to the monitors. "At least fifteen men when we arrived and an additional two came a few minutes after us."

"Zane and Noelle, check the special area in the basement for the wedding items. Enter the building carefully. At least nine men are still in the warehouse searching through crates." To the team, he said, "Remember, the goal is to get the employees out safely first then deal with the intruders."

Panic flashed through her like an electric shock at the thought of going in. She wanted to remain in the van and out of sight. The last thing she needed was to run into Dom.

"Did anyone contact Violet to find out where she's storing the items?" Zane asked.

Noelle touched the weapon holster to her waist. "I did but I haven't gotten an answer yet."

"You know the area Roc's referring to." Zane slid the door open.

She nodded, then took one more glance at the monitor to check the location that Dom and his partner were searching. Zane led the way to the building and checked the entry before letting Noelle go in front. She moved to the right, knowing Dom was on the left side of the structure then trotted down the stairs.

The hallway was dimly lit. This space wasn't as large as the area above. It held several rooms, but the corridors were short, except for the one they slowly made their way down. Two men appeared in front of her. Noelle's heart stilled as she recognized Dom's outfit. She held a hand up to Zane, then hopped into the doorway.

Zane quickly followed suit as two men stepped into the hallway ahead.

Noelle pressed her back against the wall while Zane peered out.

"Where did she go?" someone said.

"Probably hiding. Let's get out of here," Dom replied.

Zane ducked back into the alcove.

Noelle could only assume they'd looked in his direction as she prayed they would take the stairs to the left and not the ones they had come down. She was glad their assignment was to find the wedding items or Zane would've probably engaged with them.

"Someone else is conducting business tonight." Dom's deep timbre filled the air again. "Let's not get in the way."

"Big Mike."

"Exactly," Dom replied.

Zane whispered, "I wonder what that's about."

Noelle refused to say a word for fear Dom would hear her. She listened for the sounds of their feet retreating, hating that she allowed Dom to frighten her. However, she knew Talon sending Dom to find her and Shanay was an "agree to the request" or die situation. Was she willing to die not to comply? She wasn't sure. Her phone vibrated in a pocket. She retrieved it and glanced at the message.

After a few moments of silence, Zane turned toward Noelle. "You okay?"

She held up the phone, so he could see the location of the Reyes items. The last thing she wanted to do was lie to him, but she didn't feel like explaining what was bothering her.

"Roc. We're in front of the room with the targeted items." Zane shifted toward the door and twisted the knob.

Noelle kept an eye out as Zane entered the room then followed him inside. Most of the boxes' lids were off and contained various vases. Several crates in the back were open as well but two particular ones caught her eye. They didn't look like any of those boxes or crates.

She rushed over and unsuccessfully attempted to pry the lid from one. "Zane, a little help." Noelle pointed to the crowbar she'd just noticed was hanging on the back wall.

Zane did as she asked, then popped the top of the crate to reveal a variety of weapons. "We found it."

"*Now* them going after Violet makes sense," Noelle said as Zane examined one of the guns then set it back down.

"Zane and Noelle, clear the area," Roc announced as Zane went to open the next crate. "We detained all but four and they're coming your way."

Zane's body froze as if he was debating whether to follow the order.

Noelle had seen the warehouse layout and knew what would come next. "He's right. We'll get boxed in if we don't move."

"Let's go." Zane dropped the crowbar on the crate and retrieved his gun.

Noelle trailed him to the door. They needed to make it to the stairs quickly. All the other corridors were dead ends.

As Zane peeked out, the sound of gunfire erupted in the air. "Two hostiles coming down the left staircase. Next time I shoot, get to the other stairs."

Zane fired, hitting one man in the shoulder as she sprinted to the stairs. The two men raced down the hall, and Noelle pulled the trigger several times, giving Zane a chance to reach the stairs. She pivoted to go up the treads, but two men appeared at the opening. "Get off the stairs," she screamed as she vaulted over the rail to the ground.

"Linc has probably already sent back up," Zane reassured as he crouched next to her under the staircase.

The men raced toward them. Noelle wasn't sure there was enough time with them trapped with nowhere to go. Zane peeked out, firing at the nearest man. He ducked back in as bullets rained down on the small hallway.

"We need to save our bullets and shoot when they get closer."

"Got it." Noelle braced herself on the metal next to Zane, knowing they would have to step past them to get a good shot. The slow footsteps of the men were torture as she waited for the bullets.

She exhaled when law enforcement announced themselves, but didn't holster her weapon until she heard at least four items thud to the ground. If Dom actually got swept up with Big Mike's people, maybe it would buy her enough time to figure how not to work for Talon without getting killed by Dom.

The officers made quick work of arresting their attackers who were already asking for their lawyers.

"It's been a wild evening," Zane said as they headed out the exit. Glancing at her, he asked, "Noelle, is everything all right?"

"Yeah. Yeah." Noelle lifted the edges of her lips slightly, but she was searching for the Yukon in the parking lot. A police paddy wagon blocked her line of sight. "Like you said, it was a crazy night."

"I'll drop you off at your car then stop by and visit Harris and his friend at the hospital." Zane flashed his Crossroads badge as a cop approached them while they headed to his vehicle.

Noelle scanned the men being loading into the back of the truck and the crowd that gathered looking for Dom's face. She slid into the passenger seat, then they pulled out, following a couple of police cars. "When my friend told me about a gangster's daughter stealing a shipment from her father to force him to do something insane for her wedding." Noelle chuckled. "I thought the story was crazy … but then I thought about Violet."

"What else did she say?"

An explosion rocked the police convoy in front of them. Two black SUVs approached from either side of the intersection and several armed masked men jumped out carrying assault rifles. The Crossroads' team turned their cars in between the truck transporting the first set of criminals.

Had they launched a rocket in the middle of the last two law enforcement vehicles?

Noelle was surprised that the lead car and the paddy wagon had kept going.

"What the …." Zane slammed on the brakes trying to avoid the chaos.

Other Crossroads agents' and cop vehicles that were still in the vicinity of the warehouse sped toward the scene. An officer stepped out of the damaged vehicle and fired two shots before the assailants riddled him with bullets.

"Fall back," Roc called out. "They have armor-piercing rounds."

Zane threw the vehicle in reverse.

"They're stealing the evidence," Noelle yelled as if Zane couldn't see the men taking the crates with the weapons.

She had been hoping that evidence would make it hard for Dom to find a loophole out of the situation if he was caught in Big Mike's mess. Now he'd probably be back out on the streets hunting for her within hours.

"Don't worry. Roc put trackers on the crates. So, SWAT or our heavy armor team will take them down." Zane placed a hand over hers. "Regardless. Violet and her team will be safe."

But am I?

CHAPTER 14

The morning started with a jolt when Noelle answered the phone and Mia yelled for her to pack up. The team was in place to confirm extraction points. To say that her being a part of the "on the ground" team shocked her was an understatement. While she had done several security details on missions like these, she was purely remote logistics, rarely boots on the ground on an assignment of this magnitude. Now, twenty hours later, she said a quick prayer for a miracle as they prepared to jump from a plane. She hoped no one would have to sacrifice their life to save another.

Noelle scanned the diverse faces of the other people who were also in the upper level of the plane that reminded her of a luxury jet. Some slept, while others were working.

For a moment Mia stared at her watch, then stood and looked down at Calvin. "We'll be there in twenty."

A few seconds later, Noelle followed them down to the no-frills nuts-and-bolts lower level of the plane. She glanced at Zane, who moved toward Mia and Calvin. They were manning an information console setup in the center. Noelle bypassed them and heading to the area with the cargo boxes and equipment. After confirming for what seemed like the fifteen hundredth time that each personnel bag was properly packed, marked, and everything was where it should be, she made her way to the group that had grown in number.

"We need to get into Ajid undetected with our equipment and minimum interference. The Arabian will allow us to do this." Calvin nodded to the white devices that sat near the airplane's hatch.

The Arabian was the hovercraft that Calvin had altered with a cloaking ability to give them a chance of not getting shot out of the sky.

Mia put her focus on the five people who were signed for this dangerous operation. "Remember, everyone on this mission does not have an Emperor's suit," she said, referring to the technology that made the wearer appear invisible to the naked eye.

"Which means this will not be as easy as walking in and coming back out as though this is a Sunday stroll in the park," Calvin added as he handed out face masks and goggles.

"Noelle, it's time to pack up the units," Mia announced.

"On it." Noelle swiftly moved toward the already prepped and packed supply bags.

Zane trotted to catch up with her. "I'll help you."

"Thanks." Noelle grabbed four bags, and Zane took the rest which included the extra ones Daron had requested for a separate mission.

He glanced down at her shaking hands. "Are you nervous?"

"A little freaked out, but it's not only about the mission." She closed the lid on the storage unit to the Arabian, making sure she clasped it tight. "Mia told my mom about me coming overseas."

Zane moved with her to the next one. "What did she say?"

"She wants to talk and exchange Christmas gifts when I return. And, she said she loved me," Noelle said, having no desire to discuss what would happen if Talon continued to insist on

75

restoring her position in Rafael's inner circle. Dom hadn't needed to find a loophole. He and his partner must have left before the Crossroads team could snatch them up. "My mother rarely snapps out of her depression before the twenty-sixth of December."

"It's not a bad omen," Zane reassured as they headed back in Mia and Calvin's direction. "Sometimes realizing you may not have another opportunity to say what you need to say helps people cut through their excuses."

Noelle needed to hear those words. Her mom's tone made her feel like she wasn't expecting her to make it back. Instead of taking it as concern, she'd felt it was an insult. As if Noelle would mess up, as she had in the past. With Talon sending Dom to hunt Rafael's people down she didn't need a reminder of why she needed a second chance with the family. It still disturbed her that Talon had sent his top enforcer after her. She wasn't ready to psychoanalyze why. While she didn't want to die on the mission, she preferred that to dying by Dom's hands.

Zane touched her shoulder, and she turned to look at him. "Are you sure you're alright?"

"Yeah." She smiled, but he didn't seem reassured. "All bags are loaded," Noelle said as they reached the group.

"Roc and I will be in control of the Arabians until you reach the mode where you're hovering only a few feet off the ground." Mia led the group over to the devices. "At which point Calvin takes over the control and shifts the devices to landing mode."

Zane slid onto the hover pod that looked like a cross between a jet ski and a motorcycle with a square storage box on the back.

"It's very important to maintain your locked-in position until you reach the destination," Mia reminded them as she stood near Calvin in the launch area. "Small movements are alright, but sudden large ones will be problematic." She looked at Noelle who said, "Got it," before placing the goggles over her eyes.

Noelle waited until Zane buckled himself in, clicked his feet into the lock mechanism, pulled out the armrest, slid his limbs in, and engaged the safety. Once he did, she sat behind him.

"Everyone locked in?" Calvin walked around doing a quick check. "Noelle, please buckle up." He pointed down at the feet clips and pulled up the seatbelt from the back.

She put her feet in, then pulled the harness around her waist and clicked it into the lock in the front. "All buckled up for safety, sir." She saluted Calvin and he nodded in return.

"For those who have a rider on the way back, remind them to do the same." Mia claimed a seat on her machine. "The last thing we need is to help them escape Ajid then have them fall off the Arabian on the way to safety. Ready?"

"Yes, sir," everyone replied in unison.

The hatch inched open, and the warm night air entered the aircraft. Zane and Noelle were launched under Roc's control. The pod lifted from the plane's metal floor and glided into the night sky. Mia and Nicco guided theirs out, along with empty ones.

The hatch slowly closed. The Arabians descended smoothly. Noelle's heart raced as she felt herself being lifted from the seat. She tightened her grip, jerking Zane in the process.

"What's wrong?" Zane asked at the same time as Roc. The craft suddenly spun in a circle.

She didn't respond since she was trying to figure out if she could reinsert the safety belt. If she lost her grip in the attempt, she was a dead woman.

"Noelle, just put a death grip on my waist," Zane explained. "It caught me off guard."

"Cuz, what's going on?" Mia asked with concern in her voice.

Flashes of memories flooded her mind of all the times she wished she could have done things differently, like checking that her seatbelt was secure as she had done with the gear.

"Noelle?"

She felt embarrassed to answer but had no choice. "Evidently I didn't fully engage the seatbelt."

"Damn," Mia muttered. "Breathe. Zane, focus on relaxing and keeping your body position."

"Engaging emergency protocol," Roc announced as the unit finally stopped spinning.

Noelle could feel a movement up her back.

"I'm going to need you to loosen your grip on Zane a bit," Roc instructed in a gentle tone. "Tell me when you have."

She hesitated and reminded herself to trust the team, while slackened her grip. "Done."

"Is there space in between you and Zane?" Roc asked, as if he wasn't convinced.

"Yes." Not much, but there was space. Seconds later, a piece of machinery slid along her waist and clicked.

"Mia, we're good," Roc announced. "She's locked in."

"Gracias." Noelle rested her head on Zane's back and sighed with relief.

She was a little nauseous but grateful as the thumping of her heart subsided. Noelle had let old insecurities get in the way. When Calvin called her out for the seat belt incident, she quickly did it and made light to get the focus off her and any feelings of inadequacy. That defense mechanism had served her well so many times at family functions, but today it almost cost her life. Noelle had to remind herself this team wasn't judging her. They were only trying their best to make sure everyone made it home safely.

CHAPTER 15

"*T*here's a complication. The father won't leave until he knows his daughter, Kamala, is in a better place."

Zane never liked hearing those words when on an assignment. A group of armed men roamed the Ajid streets as Zane watched for the right moment to cross and enter the building where Daron had told everyone to gather. The men weren't the only danger surrounding them; it was also the people who were desperate for food and money. Stories of people selling their kidneys and children for cash to settle debts were difficult to hear.

Mia's voice entered his ear. "Are you sure the uncle took her?"

Zane assumed Mia was talking to Alia's father, Nasir, and was a little frustrated he couldn't hear both sides of the conversation.

"Stay close to me." He glanced back at Noelle, wondering if having her in the middle of the action, instead of the command center was the best decision. Zane would be heartbroken if anything happened to her.

Noelle nodded. They assigned everybody someone to extract. Roc and Mia's focus were assisting Nasir. He and Noelle were supporting Daron and Dro on their special part of the mission and escape. Right now, it sounded like the assignments were changing, and he needed to hear everything.

The minute the armed man turned the corner, he signaled for Noelle to run. They raced across the street and entered the mustard colored door.

"Nice of you to join the party." Daron greeted them as they entered the small home with modest furnishings.

"Mia, it's time to get everyone to the extraction point." Daron slipped a communication device into his ear.

Dro walked over to the older man. "Nasir."

"I will not leave without making sure she has a fighting chance to survive." Nasir reached out and took a small duffle bag off a nearby table. "Despite what she's done to fall out with her sister, I am still her father. Get her to the safer town and let Allah decide her fate from there."

"We will do our best." Dro took the bag.

"Promise me," Nasir pleaded. "He's desperate, don't let her uncle get away with this. Now that he's been excommunicated by the leader of the tribunal, he's already probably stolen her kidney."

Zane listened intensely as Daron gave a brief update on the opposite side of the room. The sister was missing from Oded and they suspected her uncle took her in order to sell her kidney to provide money to buy food for himself. The uncle had fallen on hard times after not being able to keep his word to powerful people. If Kamala returned to Oded, Nasir was convinced he'd kill her. Nicco was currently heading where they believed he took her and was supposed to meet them at the last point.

"Nasir," Dro looked over his shoulder at Mia and held up an index finger. "Nicco is already out there trying to make that happen but your refusal to leave is only making it more difficult for us to honor that request."

"Fine." Nasir picked up his things and moved toward Mia and Roc.

"Hopefully, by the time we complete the original mission,

Nicco will be at the rebel house with Kamala when we get there." Daron slipped on a device that covered his entire right forearm, then approached Noelle, who was helping Mia. "What's the quickest route to drop the aid?"

Mia gave a two-finger salute to Daron before exiting.

"Medicine first, then the food, and the cash, which would be closer to our exit." Noelle stepped closer to Daron and Zane.

"How long will that take?" Zane asked, knowing it wasn't the original route they discussed.

She didn't have time to answer as Dro asked, "Wouldn't it be quicker to deliver the food here then the medicine in the next province?"

Noelle whipped out a tablet. "This area was hit by an earthquake and crumbled buildings will block our path. Dropping off the meds will…"

"Trust the woman to do her job. If Mia hadn't mentioned she'd created a map for tracking resources and known check points, this mission would've been ten times harder." Daron looked at his watch.

Dro held his hand up in surrender as Noelle finished explaining the route.

"Copy that." Zane handed Daron two of the bags.

The Kings' mission to leave a place a little better than they found it, despite the personal risk, impressed Zane. Dro was providing help to the people of Ajid, even though it decreased their chances of getting out uninjured and alive.

"Why are we giving the food here?" Dro pointed to a building closer to the hospital.

Noelle zoomed out using two fingers. "The bag with the green label will get them through a couple of nights, but if we dropped it off here, the flat roof has enough depth not to be seen from the street. When we activate the beacon, the drone will fly in, drop off the crate full of food and it should be out of sight if they can't get to it immediately."

"It also looks like the building has a hatch to access the roof where the other one doesn't," Zane added, glancing at his watch. Dro and Daron planned to continue to send supplies to those locations once they were safely out of Ajid, as long as the government didn't compromise those places. At the rate they were going, they would not make the extraction.

"We made it." Mia's voice echoed in his ear.

"The timer has started." Daron shifted one bag onto his back while carrying the other in his hand. "Dro take the lead now that you know the route. Zane, watch Noelle's back."

He nodded as Dro opened the door to see a man in tattered clothes with a rifle.

Zane immediately pushed Noelle behind him as Dro crept backwards into the room. "Did you think I would just let you take my family away?"

"Your brother's family chose to leave with us." Dro's hand inched toward his weapon as he moved closer to Daron.

Daron pulled out a Beretta. "If you shoot him, you're dead."

"You Americans always want to play hero." He shifted the rifle in Daron's direction, then back in Dro's.

Zane nudged Noelle. "At the count of three, I need you to drop low and aim at anything hostile coming your way," he whispered, focusing on the door and windows. "We have someone else at the door."

"And what part did you play in your family's need to leave," Daron said, as Dro advanced toward the man who was backing up. "But all Americans are not bad. Just like you don't want to be judged by your new government or for your previous mistakes, don't judge us by ours."

Zane crept closer to the entry, doing the countdown with his fingers.

As soon as the door opened, Zane slammed a fist into the man's face as he entered, then kneed the hand with the gun. He ducked the man's jab and Zane followed up with an uppercut. The man grabbed him in a big bear hug. As they tussled, Zane retrieved a pen from his cargo pants pocket and stabbed the sleep agent into his thigh.

Noelle shot at the third man crossing the threshold into the house, and he retreated with the speed of lightning. Zane nodded his thanks and turned around as the uncle slid to the floor. Dro had taken the rifle and was walking away. The uncle, sprawled on the floor, raised a handgun and fired.

Before Zane could move, Daron jumped in front of Dro, and the bullet ripped into him. Noelle hopped to her feet and dashed over to them as Zane raced to disarm the uncle before he could take another shot.

CHAPTER 16

Zane had never been so relieved that Daron had been wearing bulletproof attire, despite the appearance of being in regular clothing. His heart stopped an entire minute, while he waited for Noelle to say Daron was fine.

He shook off thoughts of what happened hours earlier and prepared to knock out the final mission. The first two, at the hospital and the restaurant that had become a food center to the community after Nasir's business closed, only had minor problems, unlike the incident they had when leaving the house. Zane hoped this last one would be the same as he focused on the dark street with only a sprinkling of people.

"I activated Nicco's tracker. He's here…" Daron glanced down at the device on his forearm. "…in the house across from the back road."

Dro navigated to the last of the row houses, then held a hand up for everyone to stop as they neared an unexpected checkpoint. Dropping cash to the female rebels was turning out to be more of a challenge.

"Do you think they found them?" Zane asked, wondering if the new government had discovered the group who were fighting for change. The rebels were helping to educate girls who were not allowed back in school and women who were forced to leave their jobs when the new regime came into power. He heard stories of the soldiers going door to door looking for them.

"We'll check." Daron slipped the Beretta into his waistband, then slid next to Dro. "Your suit still works, right?"

When Dro nodded, Daron handed him a pair of glasses. Both men placed on the eyewear and touched their wrists. They disappeared before Zane's eyes. He'd heard about the Emperor's Suit, but he'd never seen it in action.

"Wow," Noelle whispered, leaning closer to his ear. "I thought Mia was blowing smoke up my rear about The Emperor's Suit. I've seen Calvin's inventions, but I thought that one was folklore."

Zane held a finger to his lips and pressed her against the wall as a few men moved closer.

"They're here," Daron confirmed. "As soon as you see an opening, come in. Time is running out. The women are leaving because soldiers are heading their way."

"We're on the move," Zane said, as armed men knocked on a door several houses away. "What's the quickest route around?"

Noelle pulled out her tablet and pointed at the screen. Zane prompted her to move in that direction with a gentle push, not liking how the man who stepped out of his home and into the street was watching them.

"We need to get her out first," Daron announced, the moment they entered the rear door. He pointed down at Nasir's daughter stretched on the rug-covered floor. "Zane, carry her. Nicco guided him safely to the extraction point."

Zane lifted the woman, who was gripping her side. Nicco took the bag from Daron which contained clothes, some money, and medicine, then pulled out his weapon.

"She just had her kidney removed so..." Nicco let the sentence linger, knowing he'd understand as he led Zane into the night. Not even five-minutes later, they arrived at an Arabian.

Nicco slung the bag over his head and shifted to the left side. Zane helped the woman on after Nicco locked himself in, and fastened the seatbelt around her, then tugged, making sure it was tight. He didn't want her to have an incident like Noelle. "You're good."

"I'll drop her at a women's shelter several towns over and out of Ajid's government's reach." His hovercraft lifted from the ground. "I should be back before extraction time."

Nicco zoomed away at a high speed.

Zane didn't even know the device could move that fast. He sprinted back to the house. A few more ladies were inside when he returned. "What do you need from me?"

"Put the beacon up on the roof. As long as they find the house empty, the girls will return." Daron slid the last bag off his back, which contained currency and the beacon notification device and handed it to the tallest of the group.

Noelle peered out of the window. "We need to get moving."

Daron ushered the women out through the door. "Noelle, go with them, then follow Dro to the extraction point."

He assumed Dro was out watching over the women to make sure they escaped safely. Zane didn't like the idea of the women carrying funds that many people would kill over, going out alone.

"Don't worry," Daron said as if he read Zane's thoughts. "I'm heading out behind them. Now get to moving."

Zane raced up the stairs and opened the hatch. The girls had lined several cement blocks up in the roof's corner. He positioned the beacon between the edge of the building and the hatch where there was a clearing, but couldn't get it to activate. He flipped the switch on and off again. Still nothing. Pulling out his flashlight, he noticed a little stone wedged in the switch. He took out his blade and used the tip to get it free.

"We need you off the roof ASAP," Daron commanded.

He planted the beacon and rushed to the hatch. A few stairs down, he heard several footsteps racing toward him. "I have an exit problem." Zane hustled to the roof.

"You're going to have to jump." Noelle's calm, even tone didn't hide the hint of panic in her tone.

"Leave without me," Zane said, preferring death by bullet than feeling every bone in his body break before taking one last breath.

"This is not up for debate. Do as she instructed," Daron demanded.

"Yes, sir." Zane peeked over the edge at the street below. "Which side?"

He prayed they had a plan. The building was too far from the other structures. That's probably why the women chose to give themselves time to escape.

"East side."

He dashed to the east wall, looking over the side again, hoping to see something there to cushion his fall. He would aim for the dirt pile. Zane moved to the opposite wall and counted down to make the run, when he heard Noelle screaming in his ear. "Put on your goggles."

Zane grabbed one of the cement blocks and placed it over the hatch just enough to give it some resistance but not enough to block entry. He slid on the goggles and positioned himself to run, then saw Noelle on the Arabian. Zane ran and jumped, aiming for the back. As he landed on the vehicle, his weight caused the Arabian to spin. He held onto Noelle until the circular movements stopped. The emergency seat belt was engaged, and he relaxed his hold on the device.

The men burst through the hatch with assault rifles pointing in every direction. Zane relaxed, knowing that they couldn't see them. He hadn't realized that the only reason he could see the other machines was because of the goggles. He felt a little silly that it had not registered in his mind that riders of the Arabian would be cloaked as well. Daron guided the device back to the extraction point and onto the plane, which was just outside the border of Ajid.

Now they had to make it to London to shower and change while the plane refueled, then get him to Chicago in time for the wedding. Zane prayed that no other incidents occurred, and the weather cooperated. His thought went to the women they left behind.

"What's on your mind?" Nicco asked as they locked the Arabian in place for the trip home.

As he watched Dro make his way up the stairs to the upper level, relief flooded Zane's system. "I was surprised we didn't try to rescue the ladies who helped Dro hide."

"Dro honestly didn't want to leave them behind, but he couldn't force them to go, either." Nicco leaned on the Arabian, after securing it in place. "He had to accept everyone doesn't want to be saved. Some people want to stay, fight, and make an impact where they are."

CHAPTER 17

"*D*ro needs to make it to the church in one piece." Noelle had a tight grip on the dashboard as Nicco sped through Chicago's South Loop as though the limo was on fire.

Nicco chuckled. "You're lucky I convinced him to let me drive." He pulled up to the beautiful stone Catholic Church, two blocks down from the hotel hosting the reception.

The limo's back door flew open and Dro hopped out before Nicco put the vehicle in park. Noelle hopped out, running to catch up with the group. Her job, along with Mia's, was to ensure Lola wasn't in the area so that Dro wouldn't see her when he entered. Even though the two had video chatted last night when he finally touched American soil, Noelle was sure they were ready to see each other in person after Dro's ordeal.

"That way." Mia pointed Noelle down the hallway as she blocked Dro from entering the second set of doors with Nicco and Daron's assistance.

Noelle took long strides toward the beautiful woman wearing an ivory wedding dress with a lace and gemstone train that accentuated her curvy body. The bride, with her brown hair 'swept into a neat bun with little diamond-studded lotus flowers inserted, paced the area at the end of the hall. Lola's good friends, Alia, Michelle, and Sydney along with Kathy, the wedding coordinator, seemed to be taking turns keeping her from making her way to the front entrance.

"Lola, he's here." Noelle smiled as Lola's movements stilled, and her face lit up with a mix of joy and relief.

Kathy surged forward as Lola's body seemed to cave.

"I'm fine." She waved everyone off.

"We just need you to step out of sight so Dro can get into place." Noelle caught Mia's "hurry and wrap it up" look.

Lola nodded, and Kathy closed the door. Noelle gave Mia the thumbs up and Dro rushed in to take his place at the altar. Noelle found it funny that Dro had wanted the wedding during the Christmas holiday, which took some wrangling since normally the Catholic Church didn't host weddings at Christmas, but when he got trapped in Ajid, Lola moved the wedding over Kwanzaa, which was the date *she* originally wanted. Once the groomsmen crossed the threshold, Mia closed the doors behind the men.

Noelle opened the doors to the ante room and the wedding planner exited followed by one bridesmaid. She swallowed to unblock the emotion swelling in her throat, happy to see the exhaustion and fear that threatened to drag the bride to her knees were gone. Lola's eyes glittered with joy and a hint of disbelief as she skimmed the pearls lining the strap of her gown with one finger. Like a second skin, the ivory lace flowed over her curves and cascaded in a sea of shifting colors around her feet. Her makeup, though understated, was flawless.

Alex Bugnon's "Missing You"—a jazzy instrumental—flowed into a soulful ballad of "Loving Me for Me". Words that meant much to Lola. Alia, the matron of honor, placed the bouquet of white roses and orchids in her trembling hands. They were tied with a blue satin ribbon trimmed with little pearl-studded lotus flowers that matched the ones in her hair and dress.

"Just a few minutes more and you'll be in his arms," Noelle said as Sydney, the jeweler who designed the wedding rings, grabbed a small satin pouch which she assumed held essential items for the bride.

"I'm so scared," Lola whispered as a tear spilled from the corner of her eye.

"Of what? Noelle snagged a tissue from the table situated in the foyer of the church, next to an ivory guest book, and dabbed away the liquid emotion. Lola's father peered into the ante room and Noelle signaled to give them a moment.

Alia moved toward Lola. "You still want to marry him, don't you?"

"More than ever. It's just ..." Lola looked up at the mosaic ceiling and blinked back more tears. "He never breaks a promise and wouldn't tell me what was going on. I could have been a widow before I ever was a bride and ..."

Alia gave Lola a gentle squeeze. "I doubt it."

"Why?"

Noelle felt like an interloper witnessing this intimate moment between friends.

"He took to land, air, and sea to come back to you," Alia said, succinctly summing up the dangerous series of events that had taken Dro from being held hostage overseas and the Kings of the Castle's efforts at making sure he made it here on this special day.

"Now if that's not a big ol' declaration of his love," Sydney chimed in. "I don't know what is."

"I could have lost him."

"But you didn't." Noelle reminded. "He's here and waiting to spend the rest of his life with you." She glanced at her watch. *Where is the rest of the bridal party?*

Lola dabbed her tears and smiled. "You're right."

"Now quit stalling. You know how Bishop Sesvalah gets when

we dawdle." Alia released Lola and stepped away as the rest of the bridal party arrived.

"I love you, but I'm not getting put in time out for you again for being late or anything else," she said with a conspirator's grin, hoping the crack would elicit a laugh from the bride.

Noelle bit her lip to contain the laughter. "Ladies, you can get in position." She held the door open for the bridal party.

Lola returned a watery smile. "You were the slow poke, as I recall. And besides, it was only once, and I was barely involved. You were the one who broke that window."

"And I only had two speeds back then—slow and stop." Alia playfully bumped the bride with her hip as they exited. "Plus, I broke that stained glass window because you dared me, talking about how it was made of candy just like the gingerbread house in Hansel and Gretel."

Noelle followed the bridal party towards the sanctuary's main doors.

Lola stifled a giggle, then peered through the small rectangular window that gave a view into the sanctuary. Several attendees were glancing in their direction, trying to get a sneak peek at the bride.

"I'll get the door," Noelle said, as the wedding planner lined the bridal party up. She held open one French door.

The flower girl was ushered in by the wedding planner. She made it halfway down the white runner before realizing mommy was on the opposite end of the aisle. The raven-haired cutie did a complete one-eighty turn, hightailing it as fast as her chubby little legs could carry her to Camille. Petals barely made it onto the streamer because she picked up speed and they took flight.

Her actions elicited chuckles and laughter from the guests as the ring bearer watched her progression and almost did the same. His father beckoned him forward, and the youngster tried to keep in time with the music, but it was obvious he wanted to make a mad dash to the finish. When the guests applauded, he stopped, put the pillow down and clapped too.

"That's right, baby. Clap for yourself," Dro's mother teased."

The room filled with laughter as the organist stopped playing "Ave Maria" as the last bridesmaid reached the alter and switched to "With You. I'm Born again" by Billy Preston and Syreeta. Noelle opened the second door so both were open for the grand entrance,

Lola's father joined them, distinguished in a tailcoat, and walked to the opening of the French doors with stained-glass windows. Everyone in the sanctuary stood. Lola stepped inside on her father's arm, and a hush fell over the crowd. In the soft glow of the flickering candles that lined the aisle, the gemstones adorning her gown twinkled like a fairytale scene brought to life. The fresh carpet of red and white rose petals released their heady fragrance as she floated down the aisle.

"Mission accomplished." Noelle smiled as Mia walked over to where she stood. She shifted to get a better look at Dro and couldn't help but smirk as he moved away from where the groomsmen were lined up and stepped directly in the center aisle, in front of the bishop. He walked toward the first pew then stopped, his eyes glistening as Lola glided through the door with her father.

"Almost," Mia whispered and frowned. "I need you to go over to the reception area to help Violet. Since she was behind in making the arrangements after what happened at the warehouse, Violet and her team are down to the wire trying to get fully set up."

Disappointed she wouldn't be able to see the entire ceremony, Noelle's shoulders dropped slightly.

"We need all the vendors cleared out of the hallway before transportation drops off the guests." Mia gave her an apologetic smile.

Mia pulled toward the entrance. "You need to get going."

"Can I just stay to see the beginning of the exchange of vows?

With the guests attending the reception it gives us a little more time for set up before the dinner portion." Noelle pressed both palms together in front of her lips.

"Fine." Mia pulled out her phone from a clutch as she guided Noelle off to the side. "The moment after, I need you exiting this door and hauling as …" Mia glanced at the statue of Mary. "… behind down the block."

Noelle opened the door and glanced back at her cousin, who hadn't entered yet. "What are you doing?"

"Calling someone to assist you." She waved her off, putting the phone to an ear.

Noelle entered the packed church, where only a few spaces were left and none of them were on the end, so she was on the side wall next to a woman handing out programs.

Lola's father took his seat as she and Dro took the spotlight. Dro looked dashing in a black tuxedo and blue shirt, as did the groomsmen. Each man cut an imposing figure, even with butterfly bandages taped to a few of their faces. On any other day, they would have looked like a band of rag tag knights fresh from the fight. But in that soft light, the only things missing from the Kings of the Castle were their crowns.

The wisdom of the ages seemed to be reflected in Bishop Sesvalah's dark brown eyes as she stood in front of the couple, serene in a purple and gold sheath and matching head wrap. Lola handed her bouquet to Alia before facing Dro, a man with olive complexion, a ruggedly handsome face and dark hair. He beamed as he planted a kiss on the back of her hand.

"I was getting worried," he teased. "I thought you were going to be late."

"Says the man who missed the rehearsal dinner he planned and was one month, five days, and ten hours late."

"And eight seconds. We mustn't forget the precious seconds," he insisted. "But you got your wish. I wanted this to happen on Christmas."

"Well, it made sense given that—"

Sesvalah cleared her throat and leaned forward. "And if you two don't stop bickering, I'll make you stand in separate corners on one foot."

Dro's best man, Shaz threw up his hands and cosigned. "You two are definitely on your own."

Sesvalah scowled at Shaz, and his smile disappeared. "And that goes for you, too, young man. You're never too old for the corner." She turned her focus to the couple. "Now, where were we?"

"Getting married, Ma'am." Dro lowered his head to keep from laughing.

Noelle fell back onto the wall laughing. She went silent when Sesvalah gave them a small smile and spoke again.

"What you two are about to embark on is more than a party and a honeymoon. Marriage is a sacred pact between you, the creator, and yourselves. It is not for the faint of heart. From this day on, think of your union as a ministry because it is."

Gesturing toward Dro and Lola, she continued, "I understand the couple have written their own vows."

Dro reached behind him and Vikkas extracted a slip of paper from the breast pocket of his tuxedo and handed it over.

"I, Alejandro Reyes, do take you, Lola, as more than the woman who will share my name. I promise to love you from this day until my last. You've been the most amazing thing that has ever happened to me and I will forever keep that in the forefront of my mind." He tucked the paper away, retrieved the blue diamond wedding ring from Daron and slid it on Lola's finger. I give you this ring as a symbol of my promise to you today, tomorrow, and forever."

Lola cleared her throat and looked up at him. "I, Lola Samuels, take you Alejandro Reyes for my husband, my lover, and my friend. Grace and mercy looked beyond my faults and saw my need and here you are, this miracle that pushes me to be a better person. Marriage is a choice that you make each second of each day. I choose you this day and each one that follows."

Someone tapped Noelle on the shoulder drawing her attention away from the couple as guests murmured awe and consent.

"Excuse me, Ms. Noelle, but your car is waiting to take you to the hotel." The young freckle-faced usher who stood close by, extended a hand toward the exit.

She held up a finger as Lola took the white gold band embedded with blue diamonds from Sydney and slipped it on his finger.

Lola stared deeply into Dro's eyes. "This is a symbol of my promise to love you in the dashes, the ones that exist between today, tomorrow, and forever."

With tears in her eyes, Noelle cast one final longing look at Dro and his bride. Noelle slipped out of the sanctuary, grabbed the hem of her gown and bolted for the steps. She had to make sure the reception was something that would never be forgotten.

CHAPTER 18

After entering the SUV, Noelle tapped the television monitor secured to the back of the passenger seat to catch the rest of the wedding on the way to the hotel. She navigated to the live streaming platform set up for those who couldn't attend.

On the screen, Sesvalah gripped their hands in hers. "Now, I have some advice before we finish here today. It's not enough to talk with one another, but you must also listen to the words that are often left unspoken. Dream and move forward together but have space where you can be alone. Never go to sleep angry. Don't waste it being mad at one another—even then. That only drives a wedge between you."

A few seconds went by as the attendees whispered their well-wishes before she added, "And when it hurts—emotionally, mentally, and spiritually; take your shoes and socks off and walk through the grass. You've heard it before, but I truly mean it—go hug a tree."

Laughter erupted around them.

"Let nature absorb your pain," Sesvalah said. "Carry the burden together, whatever it is. And love, beyond all else love, because that is the greatest miracle of all. Sesvalah nodded then looked past them to those who were there to observe the uniting of two families. "Now, as you have all witnessed the pledges of love and loyalty, I pronounce you two husband and wife. You may kiss the bride."

Dro lifted Lola's veil and cupped her face between his palms. "Here's to forever and a day," he whispered as he captured her mouth with his.

"Forever for all time," Lola countered.

And the church agreed in a rousing, "Amen."

Noelle cut the feed and raced into the ballroom. The sight of the white lotuses floating on lily pads in the pool stopped her in her tracks. The floating flowers seemed to be illuminated by a blue light. A lotus lantern with a candle in it sat at each corner. Several people were putting items in the center of the tables while others were setting plates and silverware.

"It's beautiful isn't it?"

Noelle turned to find Zane wearing a black suit, grey shirt, blue tie, and the corset vest she had given him as a not-so-secret Santa gift. He looked devastatingly handsome. "Bonito."

Zane chuckled. "I hope you're talking about the flowers being pretty and not me."

"I'm sorry. I can never remember the word for handsome in Spanish." Noelle hoped Zane didn't keep his suit jacket on all night, because it was hiding the best part of the masterpiece.

"Well, we're going to have to work on that."

"Zane and Noelle." Violet rushed over. "Time to put you to work." She looped one arm through Zane's and another through Noelle's, bringing them to where several centerpieces were situated on rolling carts.

Noelle immediately saw what the issue was when Harris lifted the round centerpiece filled with a red lotus with red crystals floating in water and crept toward the table, trying not to spill the water. Another person came to grab one with a white lotus and colorful crystals, that reminded Noelle of the gemstones on Lola's dress, and he also inched back toward the tables.

"Where do the red centerpieces go?" She stood close to the black wheeled cart.

"To the odd tables. The white goes to even," Violet explained as she picked up a centerpiece.

"Zane, that cart goes with Harris." Noelle used the tip of her shoe to unlock the wheels on the cart with the white lotuses.

"Copy that." Zane rolled the arrangement carefully, following the man who had yet to make it to his destination. "Partner your people up. If they roll the cart between four tables, each person sets two, then move on to the next grouping."

"Thank you." She waved the team over as Harris and Zane continued to place centerpieces.

Once they had their marching orders, everyone moved at top speed. Noelle partnered with the florist. "Where do these go?" She touched the tall cylinder vases with red crystals and a red lotus at the base, a pink lotus floating in the middle, and a white one just below a white floating candle.

"The tables where Castle members will sit." Violet pointed to the sign that read Knight of Bronzeville.

Noelle placed the centerpiece down on the Morgan Park table, then the South Holland, Lahaina, Hyde Park, Evanston, Kingston, Paradise Island and Devon. She had never paid attention to how many areas the Kings, Queens, Knights, and Ladies represented until now.

Violet had taken care of eight tables as well, but they still had more to go. Zane and Harris joined in, helping to place the tall centerpieces. Servers moved in between them, setting more items on the tables.

Her phone rang just as they finished the last one, and Violet rolled the cart away.

"Please tell me you're done," Mia said.

"Yes." She disconnected the call before rushing to the florist. "Did you clear the vendor hallway?"

"That's why all the centerpieces were on rolling carts provided by the hotel, to make sure our truck was out of the way in time," Violet responded as she waved her people out the vendor entrance. "I appreciate everything you've done for me." She gave Noelle a quick hug before sliding out of the exit.

Noelle sighed in relief, watching as she moved to the door leading to the guest parking and the bar area. She shut the door, wanting to take one last look at the room to make sure everything looked perfect.

Zane walked over to her. "Now Operation Lotus is officially over."

"That it is." She moved toward the pool heading to the reception area.

"Noelle, I know you want to see Dro and Lola's big entrance." He grabbed her hand and guided her on the clear pool covering. "But would you grant me one dance before the happy couple arrives?"

She looked at the banquet staff, who were still prepping the tables. "There's no music."

He pulled a phone from his jacket pocket and put on "You" by Jesse Powell, then slid it back in.

"What do you know about that?" Noelle was sure Mia had told him it was one of her favorite songs. Her mother's entire face would light up when it came on and whatever memories associated with it made her happy. That positive energy transferred to Noelle.

Zane took her in his arms, swaying to the music. "I know I'm captivated by you."

"Are you really?" Noelle smiled, realizing the best holiday gift she received was getting to know him.

He looked deeply into her eyes. "Most definitely."

When Zane's lips lowered to hers, all the chatter and clinking of silverware faded in that moment. The kiss was sweet and scorching hot at the same time. All her senses came alive causing her to consider suggesting they skip the reception. She slid both arms around him as passion swept her away.

"Mr. and Mrs. Reyes will arrive soon," a soft feminine voice said interrupting the moment and Noelle ended the kiss.

Noelle glanced back to see Chef Valentina Romano and the event manager near the kitchen entrance.

"I'll let my staff know." Valentina glanced at the food trays that the banquet staff was taking to the reception.

"I guess our time is up," Zane said as Noelle stepped out of his embrace.

"Yes. The reception hour is almost over and the bridal party should be done taking pictures at the church," Noelle took his hand as they stepped off the dance floor.

Michelle DaCosta, who had repaired the vandalized wedding dress, and Rajay Charmani who had been her bodyguard, were the first to enter when the staff opened the doors to the banquet area.

"I definitely want her to design my dress if I ever get married." Noelle made her way to their table as more guests entered the space. Her phone vibrated and she read the message from Mia.

Zane pulled out her chair, "You'll look beautiful in one of her creations." He leaned and kissed her on the cheek. "Call me when you get home, no matter how late you get in."

"Where are you going?" Noelle called out to him an shifted the seat next to her back. "Mia made arrangements for you to stay."

Minutes later, a thunderous applause and cheers filled the grand ballroom as the bride, groom, and wedding party entered to the musical sounds of "Celebration" by Kool and the Gang. Each couple with their own unique, energetic dance moves.

Noelle smiled as Dro and Lola finally made it to the sweetheart table. Daron and Cameron walked toward the table behind Noelle's group.

"Good job team." Daron acknowledged the other Kings,

Queens, and Knights as they went to their respective table. "You're officially off the clock."

"Yeah right," Noelle chuckled and looked at Mia and Calvin as they sat down next to her. "I've been around you all enough to know that if anything jumps off. Everybody will be back on duty."

"She ain't wrong," Cameron teased as Daron took the seat next to her.

Toasts and well wishes were made in honor of the couple then the three-course plated meal was served with an array of Italian and Spanish-themed dishes pre-selected by each guest.

"Valentina, did an excellent job on this food," Noelle said to Mia.

Noelle's mouth dropped as a six-tier circular wedding cake frosted with ivory buttercream and accented with lotus flowers complimentary to the decorations throughout the ballroom was rolled in.

"Oh my, this cake is beautiful," Lola said. "I don't know if I want to cut it."

Dro chuckled and sweetly kissed her. "Baby, if we don't cut it then we'll have some angry guests on our hands."

Zane laughed and leaned toward Noelle while eyeing the cake. "He's right about that one."

Lola gave Dro a sheepish smile. "It's our day so we should be able to do what we want, right?"

"You have a point, but I'd like to get out of here soon rather than manage the disappointed expectations of our family." Dro stood and extended a hand toward Lola.

Smiling, Lola asked, "Why are you in such a hurry, my husband?"

Noelle snickered. "The way Dro is looking and whispering in Lola's ear he's ready to skip to the honeymoon."

Signaling to one of Chef Valentina's culinary staff standing nearby, Lola said. "Knife, please."

The cutting of the cake was a picture-perfect moment. Noelle fully enjoyed the slice of the decadent dessert she had selected. Zane had picked a different tier so they could try two flavors. Khalil stood and walked over to the deejay and took the mic. "One last toast before the bride and groom's first dance ... well, make that the second since they came in showing off their dance moves."

Noelle and the other guests laughed then they all grabbed a glass.

"In all seriousness." Khalil turned and faced the couple. "I wish you all the best in life and love." He placed a hand over his heart. "I remember when Dro was about knee high to a grasshopper."

"Come on, dad," Vikkas teased. "He's never been a knee high to anything."

"That may be true," Khalil said, trying to hold back a smile as he swept a gaze across the nine men who became original Kings of the Castle. "But he has come so far since those days when you were students at Macro. And you all have achieved more than I could ever have imagined. And now you are choosing women who are powerful in their own right." He walked to Lola and took her hands in his. "Thank you for being his person. I can rest assured that he's in good hands just like you're in good hands. Be gentle with each other as you take this path together."

After the first dance, the evening flew by too fast for Noelle. She enjoyed spending time with Zane among people who were full of joy and happiness.

Zane took Noelle's hand leading her off the dance floor as the music slowed. "Come on."

"Where are we going?" She followed him through the tables thinking about the last few weeks.

Despite all the craziness, this turned out to be one of the best experiences. During the layover in London, she had a great talk with her mother. The mission of helping in Ajid was life changing. It made her appreciate all the things she'd taken for granted. She decided to ask for an overseas assignment to help stay off Talon and Dom's radar. By the time she was stateside again, she hoped they would have moved on and let go the idea of getting Rafael's crew back together. Noelle hoped, with everything within her, that her relationship with Zane continued to grow, even if it would be long distance for a while.

"Somewhere we can have a private dance." Zane led her out into the hallway that the vendors used and pulled her into his embrace.

She rested her head on his chest as they swayed to the sounds flowing from the ballroom. "Our dance got interrupted earlier, didn't it?"

Seconds later, Dro and Lola slipped out hand in hand making their way to the parking lot. Noelle would have waved but she doubted they saw anyone other than each other. If only Noelle could experience amazing love like that. One willing to go to the ends of the earth and back to be together, it would be an awesome thing. Maybe. One day. Glancing up at Zane, Noelle pulled him into a passionate kiss. She hoped a miracle wouldn't be needed and the stars were already aligned for their love to continue to grow and blossom. Noelle was excited to create more beautiful moments like these with Zane in the future.

KINGS OF THE CASTLE CHAPTER 1

Burning this place to the ground would be a kindness." Khalil Germaine's steps faltered for a moment, and his hands curled into fists by his side. "We should have known better. *I* should have known better."

Vikkas glanced at his father. Deep lines edged the older man's mouth, chiseled by grief and regret. "Don't say that. None of what happened here is your fault."

"Of course it is," Khalil shot back as a gust of air from the cooling system blew the tunic around his muscular form. "I built this place with my own hands. I am the one who entrusted them with my legacy for five years."

"You couldn't have known what they would do."

Khalil released a weary sigh that spoke volumes to his inner turmoil. "Wealth invites greed, and absolute power corrupts even those with the best of intentions. Every student of history knows as much—I taught you those lessons myself. I taught the other eight as well."

"That's true," Vikkas conceded, falling in step with his father as they trailed the length of the hidden passage, undetected. "But not all men are weak. You taught me that, too. Wealth and power never changed your heart."

Khalil's arm chopped through the air, dismissing his words with an angry wave. "But now my heart has come to nothing."

Before Vikkas could protest, his father veered toward the massive wall.

Vikkas shifted his weight onto the balls of his feet as nervous energy snaked up his spine. "Are you sure breaking into The Castle is a good idea? They killed Zahara, just for warning us. We should wait for the others."

"We cannot afford to wait. Her death must not be in vain." Khalil choked on the words as his fingertips slid over the cool stone as though marking their progression. "They will not give up their power so easily. By tomorrow, everything she died for could vanish."

"But the evidence—the dossiers and photos. What they did to those women ... to the *children* ... they can't explain all that away."

Khalil paused to look at Vikkas over his shoulder. "You live in a civilized world. For that, I am grateful. But you have no idea what lies beneath. The corruption that protects men of privilege runs deep—far deeper than you know."

Vikkas thought of the journal that an original Castle member had sent to their hotel room, the one that contained pages of entries that detailed all the damage that had been done. One entry in particular had aged his father nearly ten years and chilled his own blood ...

Delivered a prepubescent female submissive...trained to serve wherever and however needed. Bonus: Vocal cords are severed to ensure discretion.

And this was the mildest of the crimes that had been committed.

Vikkas frowned. "I'm not a child. Or a fool."

His father twisted far enough to clap a conciliatory hand on his shoulder. "Of course not. You are a man of principle; I am proud of that. But it also blinds you. All of you. Which is why you will need each other."

"Who?" He met his father's gaze with a mix of curiosity and annoyance. "Why these eight men? And why haven't they answered?"

"They will." For the first time that night, Khalil smiled. "They are bold, like you, especially when it comes to protecting the ones they love—shoot first, ask questions never." He took in a breath that seemed ladened with bitterness and regret. "They are still finding pieces of Zahara like flower petals cast upon an ocean of sorrow and shame. Her only crime was speaking with me about the terrible things she witnessed at the Castle."

Vikkas turned back to the wall as Khalil whispered, "The underworld came running the moment we left the States. Now you, and those eight men I summoned, are the key to The Castle's redemption. They. Will. Make. Things. Right." He looked gazes with Vikkas and added, "But to avoid unnecessary bloodshed, they should not see us—or them—coming."

Vikkas tensed and moved closer to the wall. When nothing happened, he blew a hard breath from his lips. "Is this the right place?"

"Yes. Help me." Khalil pointed to the area that had nine faint scratches on the surface. "Right here."

Khalil regarded his son in patient silence.

"Where, here?" He pressed his hands against the stone.

He nodded. "Just so. Push."

Vikkas did as his father asked. At first, he felt only the expected, perfect resistance of an impenetrable stone wall, but then something shifted. He shoved harder, and the stone gave way beneath his hands. They stepped into the night air. Someone laughed, and their progression halted. Vikkas' head swiveled in the direction of the sound. Several armed men had chosen their exit point for a smoke break.

"We have to go back to the conference room and exit through

the front." His heart quickened as he quickly ushered his father back inside.

"This passage also leads to a camera blind spot on the main level." Khalil headed in the opposite direction of the conference room.

Vikkas waited until the hidden door closed, sent off a text to their driver, and followed his father. Seconds later, his phone vibrated. "The car should be here by the time we make it to the driveway," he whispered.

Khalil cracked open the exit slightly and peered out into the main level corridor. "The hallway is clear."

They stepped out but didn't start moving until the hidden entrance closed, then walked to the front doors. Vikkas scanned the lengthy golden entrance with three red strips of carpet, two of which went up a double set of stairs and the other down the hallway in the center. Two vases filled with artfully arranged flowers on the sideboards were on either side of the opening. A long dark polished wood table used to register Castle guests, sat in the area between the foyer and the grand staircases. They were waiting in the hallway not too far from the table.

As they neared the exit, Vikkas patted his pocket and felt for the flash drive with the evidence that would set things in motion. He muttered another curse. "I left my wallet in the conference room." He had retrieved the safe's access card from it then sat it on the conference table. Vikkas couldn't leave it behind with that and their hotel keycard in it. "I'll be back."

"Be quick about it."

Vikkas pivoted, took a few hurried steps, and noticed a red light blinking rapidly as he came closer. He turned to ask his father if he'd seen it when a shadow flickered, and Khalil lunged at it.

An ambush. They were waiting for us.

That was all Vikkas had time to think before instinct took over and he bolted in their direction.

A movement to the left caught his attention moments before a massive man rushed toward him. The goon reached for a holster beneath his grey suit jacket.

Vikkas reached the registration table in two quick strides, throwing his palm down to vault himself over the table, and launching his feet toward the giant. Two large men, both armed coming for them, and his father didn't have the speed he once had. If he didn't take them both out quickly—

Don't think. Just fight.

His boots connected with the man's chest and knocked him to the ground. Vikkas had hoped the impact would dislodge the weapon from his hand, but the goon had an iron grip. Without even trying to get up, the man raised the gun and fired as Vikkas fell on him. A searing pain blazed across Vikkas' arm.

Vikkas grabbed grey suit's wrist, shoving the barrel away as the man fired off a barrage of rounds in an ear-ringing staccato. Where was his father? Was he hit? Adrenaline surged through him, and Vikkas pummeled the man in the face as hard and fast as he could.

Three punches. Four. Five. As his fist connected for the sixth time, slick, fresh blood coated his knuckles. Several more rounds went off. After the last one, Vikkas saw the man's bloody teeth glistening through a wide gap that had opened between his lip and chin. With the seventh punch, the gun finally slid away, clattering across the floor and disappearing from view as the man threw up his hands, trying to save what was left of his face.

His plan had been to grab the pistol as soon as the guy let go. But now he had no time to find where it had landed.

Not seeing the weapon nearby, Vikkas rose and issued a kick to the man's chest that knocked the wind out of him. He spotted grey suit's firearm and spun in one fluid motion, flying over the table again.

Another gun went off, and his stomach turned to ice. But no, his father was still on his feet, locked in a struggle with the other man, trying to keep his arm pointed away from Vikkas. The pistol swung back in his direction, and Khalil slammed his elbow down into the man's arm. The gun went off again, and the bullet smashed into the floor. Vikkas shifted gears, realizing going for grey suit's weapon would put him in the other goon's line of fire.

As grey suit struggled to his feet, Vikkas raced to a sideboard table, and snatched up the closest vase—a solid marble bludgeon that fit perfectly in his hand. His father was still struggling with his assailant, and then Vikkas was staring straight down the barrel of a Glock.

Grey suit must have had a second gun.

Without hesitation, he slammed the vase across the giant's head like a bat. The man hit the ground with a solid thud. He gave one last punch for good measure and was satisfied when the man's head rolled to the side, arms fell to the ground and eyes fluttered to a close.

Khalil wrestled for the weapon with a man dressed in black. Vikkas didn't wait to see who won that battle. He spun in their direction and raced toward them. Khalil tripped over the carpet's edge and gave the intruder an advantage.

When the pistol fired several shots, Vikkas couldn't see the flash. Had his father had taken the hit?

A split second later, he reached "black suit" and fell on him in a fury. Vikkas slammed the vase into his head, over and over. On the third hit, he felt the gunman's cheek give way, crushed beneath the force of his rage. With a fourth swing, the man raised his arms blindly in front of him, trying to block the blow. The crack of an upper forearm was unmistakable even over the newcomer's shouts for them to leave. The man screamed, dropped his gun, and ran out the front door, cradling his misshapen limb.

Vikkas scooped up the pistol and spun around, still brandishing the vase in one hand as he leveled the gun at the giant in the grey suit who ran up on them. He pulled the trigger, but the weapon only clicked. *Must've been damaged by the vase.*

The beast of a man stared at him, a slow, bloody grin spreading across his face. He raised the gun and aimed at his father.

Vikkas lunged in front of Khalil just before the beast fired.

Click.

He was out of ammo. Vikkas grinned back. Dropping the gun, he snatched up the second vase, launched himself at him, yelling like a maniac and waving the vase through the air.

The big guy wasn't having any part of it. With a look of raw terror, he turned tail and ran.

Father.

Vikkas scrambled to Khalil with his arm throbbing and bleeding, taking in the blood darkening the front of his father's tunic. He fell to his knees and tore the cloth apart to assess the damage. At the very least, the bullet had punctured a lung. *Had it hit his heart?* He applied pressure to the wound with one hand and snatched his phone from his pocket with the other.

Before he could make the call, running footsteps echoed behind him. He whipped his head around, about to reach for the vase, but then he saw who it was.

"I called for help. An ambulance is on the way."

"Some help you were," Vikkas growled, realizing the man had been there long enough to provide some assistance besides dialing a number.

"Stop." The command came from Khalil, his voice thready yet firm. "Protect him. He cannot be caught up in this."

"Protect him?" Vikkas huffed. "Dispatch will see the number on *their* end."

"It's a burner phone."

"Stay back." Vikkas lifted his bloody palm to warn off the interloper.

"What the hell happened?" he asked, instead of doing as he was commanded.

"Leave." He tightened his hold on his father. "Before the authorities arrive."

The man stared at the spreading stain on Khalil's tunic, his feet planted on the ground.

Vikkas swallowed hard and calmed the fear raging inside him. "No one can know you were here." He nodded toward the front door that still stood open to the night, indicating the nearby parking lot and its fleet of luxury cars. The wailing sirens blasted in a way that signaled the first responders were close. "Go. Help is on the way."

Finally, the man turned away, walking then running out the front doors.

Khalil groaned, watching Vikkas through half-closed lids. "Remember the mission. They *will* come. Tell them this: 'Evil prevails when good men do nothing.' They *are* good men, my son. The absolute best. They will come. They must. The Castle belongs to…"

His father's eyes closed, his skin turning gray, and Vikkas's heart threatened to burst from his chest. He maintained pressure on the wound, wishing he had more hands—or his own life to give.

"Father." He spoke the word through clenched teeth, barely trusting his voice. "Don't you dare die on me."

Download your copy today
https://books2read.com/Kingsofthecastle

PROMISE ME A MIRACLE SERIES

Jaxon Malone lands the simplest job of his career—travel to the Kingdom of Ajid and escort Alia Fadel back to America to be the maid of honor in their friends' wedding. But no one foresaw a previous regime suddenly surging back to power over the country —or their decision to imprison Alia for standing up to the new rulers. Silenced and alone, Alia loses hope of ever being free again.

Jax springs into action, but every attempt to get Alia out of the country fails. Things go from bad to worse when Ajid's Supreme Leader insists on marrying her in a ruthless power play of a publicly televised ceremony.

Jax needs help—and fast. Several Kings of the Castle rise to the call, traveling behind enemy lines to rescue Alia and her family. But it'll take a miracle to pull off their daring escape plan, which must happen before the new government seals the country off from the rest of the world. Is it too late, even for the Kings, to enact the impossible?

https://books2read.com/operationbutterfly

Someone is trying to kill Dr. Sydney Lomax. The award-winning jeweler and inventor accepts a special assignment from Dro Reyes: transport his custom-made wedding rings across a lake of fire. But neither is aware that the job involves mortal danger. Sydney's enemies are determined to succeed, since her mission across the sands of Durabia threatens their secret munitions dump—where a Doomsday Bomb is silently ticking.

Ethan Wakefield, tasked with finding the government's covert facility that's filled with Sydney's inventions, is assigned to protect yet use her. He must locate her tech, which could save or destroy countless lives, before time runs out. But lines get quickly blurred, and now Ethan and Sydney's newfound love is also at risk of destruction in a deadly game of cat and mouse.

As time winds down, Ethan does everything in his power to bring Sydney home alive—but this time, even his best effort might not be good enough.

https://books2read.com/Operationdiamond

Michele DaCosta, bridal gown designer extraordinaire receives the commission of her life—except that it's impossibly last-minute. On top of a stressed bride dealing with ghosts from her past, there's also a high-level blizzard attacking all of Chicago, trapping Michele with an over-protective bodyguard.

Rajay Chamani's assignment is to shield the pretty fashion designer from the stalker who ruined a family heirloom and is now determined to use Michele as a messenger to the bride. The situation intensifies when the groom goes missing in action in the Middle East, and Rajay and Michele end up being snowed in. He's blindsided by one more complication: his growing attraction to Michele, simmering hotter even as Mother Nature has the last icy laugh.

Only weeks remain before Chicago's biggest society wedding of the year. Can Rajay and Michele work together to defeat a stalker, defy a blizzard, and finish the world's most elaborate bridal gown to ensure wedding bells win over doomsday knells?

https://books2read.com/Operationivory

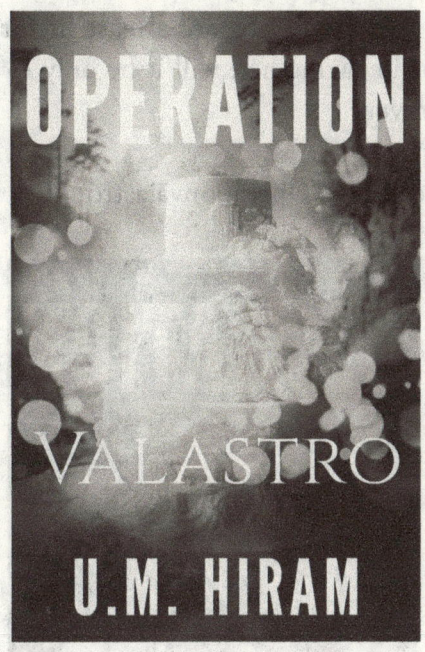

Valentina Romano, a world-famous celebrity chef, is hired to prepare the meal and signature cake for the wedding of Dro Reyes and his fiancée, Lola Samuels. But days before the celebration, she and her four specialty chefs are flat on their backs in an Italian hospital after falling eerily ill.

Dr. Marcus Kyncade, known for his advances in neurotoxins, is the attending physician for the five new patients. His attraction to Valentina is undeniable, but he's shut down by the woman's long-time business associate—and time's relentless scythe.

But to save Valentina's life, he has to beat the blade. He must win a frantic race against the clock to not only find an antidote to a mysterious poison, but also determine exactly who wants Valentina dead.

Will Valentina and her specialty chefs survive this attack from an invisible enemy in time to prepare a feast fit for a King? And if Marcus succeeds in saving her, will it be only to watch her walk out of his life forever?

https://books2read.com/Operationvalastro

Noelle Jakob is livid when she's abruptly pulled from a high-profile assignment to locate a vanished VIP bridegroom. The logistics genius for Crossroads Security, tasked with finding the event's missing florist instead, isn't any happier about having to partner with Zane Hargrave. The one man who makes it impossible for her to focus is now her key to solving this mystery and getting back to her original mission.

Easier said than done.

The closer Noelle and Zane's leads get them to their target, the deeper the danger they encounter. With the florist in trouble and the high-profile wedding fast approaching, it's going to take a holiday miracle to align the stars and ensure the event is a "full-blooming" success.

https://books2read.com/Operationlotus

KINGS OF THE CASTLE SERIES

The Castle: elite, elusive ... dangerous.

A secret organization which once stood for protection and benevolence, The Castle has now been corrupted by crime, greed, and dirty politics. Every crime syndicate and dirty politician on earth are determined to control the massive fortune guarded by The Kings: a found family forged by fate but called to action by crisis.

When their mentor ends up on the business end of an assassination attempt, nine men are summoned to right old wrongs and track those responsible. The Kings of the Castle, now grown into captains of industry and leaders of men across Chicago, bring their unique skill sets to the daring mission to bring their enemies down—even if they have to rack up a body count to do it.

The job won't be easy, and nobody knows it clearer than the women destined to love each of these men. As powerful forces conspire to twist the Castle's riches for their own good, convictions are challenged and relationships are tested. In the end, will the sacrifices be worth it?

The Kings of the Castle is a series of self-contained stories with characters in a shared world full of high-stakes suspense, fast-paced plots, and breathtaking romance. Each book is written by a national bestselling author and features a different King of the Castle.

https://books2read.com/Kingsofthecastle

Mariano "Reno" DeLuca uses his skills and resources to create safe havens for women in dangerous situations—until a surge in Chatham's criminal activity threatens the safety and anonymity for the residents of The Second Chance at Life Women's Shelter. Though Reno finally admits that the shelter must be relocated, the crisis couldn't be more ill-timed. Just when he's summoned back to The Castle to meet with his brothers in the secret society, a new woman lands on the shelter's doorstep. Immediately drawn to the mysterious beauty, he struggles to refocus on The Castle's newest challenge: an immoral takeover attempt by an enemy who's supposed to be an ally.

Zuri Okusanya, a Tanzanian Princess, has snuck into America with nothing but the clothes on her back and handwritten instructions from her deceased mother. Desperate for refuge from an arranged marriage by her politically motivated father, the princess has survived a near-death experience to land at the door of the

Chatham shelter, unwilling to trust anyone except Mariano DeLuca.

Reno is conflicted. His fugitive princess is as beautiful as she is intelligent, and her plight speaks straight to his soul—not a vulnerability he can afford with so many lives now at stake. Though he strives not to lose his heart to the forbidden goddess, destiny has other plans.

Will Mariano have the fortitude to defeat his adversaries and save the women of the shelter—now including the woman he loves —or will time win and strip him of everything and everyone he holds dear?

https://books2read.com/kingofchatham

Shaz Bostwick prides himself on his moral compass and business ethics—but both are deeply challenged from the moment Camilla Gibson walks into his office, urgently seeking his help.

Camila has no choice but to throw herself on Shaz's mercy. Though she's a renowned blogger for her world adventures and colorful modeling gigs, this is one instance that fame won't solve. Her daughter, Ayanna, needs specialized treatment in Chicago, but time—and the authorities-- aren't on her side. She's elated when the charming but tough lawyer pledges his support.

Shaz, raised as an immigrant, knows the heartache of family separation firsthand. He's moved by Camila's plight, and calls in favors as the clock ticks down. In return, he's presented with a disturbing offer: let baby Ayanna slip through the cracks in exchange for a handsome reward. The call gives him a tip about an illegal adoption ring, but he can only bust the criminals with the help of his brothers from The Castle.

Fed up with politicians and businessmen with too much money and too little scruples, Shaz mobilizes his friends with astounding speed. His tenacity and intelligence move Camila to her core, igniting an attraction she never thought she'd know again—but there's no way she can act on the sparks with the threat deportation still looming for Ayanna and her.

Shaz Bostwick has a fierce reputation for making a way when there is none—but will his legislative superpower be enough to forge a future with his adventurous Camila?

https://books2read.com/KingofEvanston

Doctor Jaidev Maharaj's life takes a dark turn when a coma patient becomes pregnant, propelling him into media infamy. His troubles are tripled when law enforcement and the government join the clamor—and that's before he learns about the attempt on his mentor's life. When he resolves to chase the details, Jai is thrust into a secret brotherhood that belongs to a world he never conceived—and a destiny that suddenly demands more than he's prepared to give.

Temple Devaughn awakens from a year-long coma to discover she has a child—whom she doesn't remember conceiving. The police suspect foul play at the medical center where she was cared for, but to find the truth Temple must trust Jai Maharaj: a stranger who may or may not have her best interests at heart.

As a dark family secret threatens to sabotage Jai and Temple's quest for the truth, they are pulled toward each other in ways they cannot deny—but betrayals, setbacks, and endless mysteries mar every attempt they make to connect. When unseen enemies conspire to silence Temple for good, true values are tested. Will Jai prove to Temple—and himself—that their love is worth fighting for?

ABOUT THE KINGS OF THE CASTLE SERIES:
Each book from 2-9 is a standalone story in the same world, with no cliffhangers.

https://books2read.com/KingofDevon

Two things threaten to destroy most of Daron Kincaid's life: the tracking device he developed to locate human trafficking victims, and an inherited membership in a mysterious outfit called The Castle.

The new developments come with awful timing. After years with Interpol and the FBI, including a sizable sting that brought down notorious criminals, Daron's ready to move on and build a new life with the love of his life, Cameron Stone. But even after years of security expertise, he's not prepared for Marquise Sinclair's treachery. The international crime boss is determined to take Daron's position in the Castle by leveraging Cameron's life against a project worth billions.

Yet even the savvy Sinclair is utterly unaware about Cameron's unique talents: her loveliness conceals highly specialized training to make men weak or put them on the wrong side of the grave. She's not the only one with secrets. When Daron hides key details from Cameron and his inner circle, the deception only complicates an already tumultuous situation.

Can Daron take on Marquise, manage his loyalty to the Castle, and keep deep confidences without permanently losing the woman he loves?

https://books2read.com/Kingofmorganpark

Real estate developer Kaleb Valentine is known for working lifestyle magic, turning failing communities into thriving havens in the Metro Detroit area. He's on track to become one of the city's most renowned success stories—until a suspicious house fire in one of his properties leaves nothing but charred wreckage and five bodies.

Suddenly in the center of an intense criminal investigation, Kaleb is forced to revisit the harsh life he barely escaped as a teen. Life gets even more complicated when he volunteers at the The Second Chance at Life Women's Shelter—and meets a woman who fascinates him like no other.

Skyler Pierson has no time for romance, let alone love—so nobody's more surprised than she when Kaleb Valentine shows up and instantly puts his charm to work on the walls around her heart. But when the dashing entrepreneur asks her for a favor, she's curious and asks questions—too many of them. The danger she'd thought long-gone from her world is back with a vengeance, worsened by mysterious influences from Kaleb's dark past, as well.

Everything is on the line. How far will Kaleb's enemies go to take him—and his new love—down for good?

https://books2read.com/u/4DDl9g

Grant Khambrel, a sexy, successful Texas architect, has worked hard to build a thriving business, only to learn that dirty strings were attached to his seed money—ties it's taken him years to severe.

When the firm wins the prestigious multi-million-dollar

contract to renovate the city's United Center, it should be a reason for celebration, but the past Grant never asked for becomes the inescapable firestorm of his present. Rumors of improper business ethics cast shadows on his company's reputation, intensified when Grant is blackmailed by a powerful local politician.

None of it's the best foot to start out on when meeting the most gorgeous woman he's ever seen.

Autumn Knight, the savvy and beautiful Administrative Director of the United Center, grew up around both sides of Chicago politics. Though her father, a powerful real estate tycoon and alderman, continues to pressure her for under-the-table kickbacks, Autumn is steadfast about her ethics—though that manifesto is harder to maintain when she meets charismatic Grant Khambrel.

The intense man, preselected by her father's committee for the Center's new project, is everything she craves and nothing she can want. Though their chemistry is overwhelming from the start, she doesn't dare trust her heart to a person with such an uncertain past. When more lies and secrets surface, exploring even a casual romance with the gorgeous architect is out of the question.

Will Grant prove to Autumn that he's hero she desires and deserves—or will his tainted success be the ruination of the future they long to believe in?

https://books2read.com/Kingoflincolnpark2

Alejandro "Dro" Reyes has been a "fixer" for as long as he can remember, which makes him perfectly suited to own a crisis management company focused on repairing professional reputations. Business in the Windy City is booming—until a mysterious call following an attempt on his mentor's life forces him to drop everything and accept a position with The Castle. Though his family has been affiliated with the secret organization for decades, his new involvement leads to being blindsided by an enemy he never saw coming.

Lola Samuels, the polished public relations maven of Chicago's elite, sets aside her growing attraction to Dro in the name of seeking assistance for her newest assignment. Longtime bad boy Shawn Mayhew needs some fast shine on his tarnished image: a simple enough job if she and Dro tag-team the essentials, right?

But sometimes, success really is in the details.

Lola is totally unaware of the animosity between the Mayhews and the Reyes —until it's too late. The cut-and-dry job is quickly spun into a sticky web of danger and deceptions—most prominently, Dro's scheme to use their working relationship to gain intel on his enemy.

When Lola discovers she's a pawn in Shawn and Dro's dangerous game, she's conflicted—yet then captured. Alejandro's carefully controlled world is thrown into chaos, and he vows to use every resource in his arsenal, including the skills of the eight men with whom he's just reconnected, to rescue the woman he desperately loves.

https://books2read.com/u/bQe9W7

Dwayne Harper's passion is giving disadvantaged boys the tools to transform themselves into successful men. But when he steps up to take his place among The Kings of the Castle—the men he considers brothers—politics and personalities clash, conspiring against him.

Tiffany Mason is also harboring a dark secret that can shatter Dwayne's ultimate dream, not to mention the depths of his heart. While Dwayne is everything she could want in a handsome, intelligent, and driven man, details from her past have her doubting her worthiness of his marriage proposal. Complicating matters are new accusations against Dwayne, testing his dedication to his cause.

Enter a female acquaintance who's determined to help Dwayne persevere, but her methods become questionable when she uses blackmail to achieve her goals—leveraging Tiffany's scandalous past in her jealousy-driven war chest. Exposed to Dwayne in this insidious manner, Tiffany has no right to recourse, and can only hope Dwayne chooses her as his queen for life.

One woman holds the key to his success; the other will guide him to the cliff of his downfall. It will be the full test of Dwayne Harper's character to discern the difference—and claim his due success as a King of The Castle.

https://books2read.com/King-of-Lawndale

ABOUT THE KINGS OF THE CASTLE SERIES:

Each book from 2-9 is a standalone story in the same world, with no cliffhangers.

https://geni.us/Kingsofthecastleseries

KNIGHTS OF THE CASTLE SERIES

No good deed goes unpunished, or that's how Ellena Kiley feels after she rescues a child and the former Crown Prince of Durabia offers to marry her. He is given nine days in order to make her fall in love with him.

Kamran learns of a nefarious plot to undermine his position with the Sheikh and jeopardize his ascent to the throne. He's unsure how Ellena, the fiery American seductress, fits into the plan but she's a secret weapon he's unwilling to relinquish.

Ellena connection to Kamran challenges her ideals, her freedoms, and her heart. Plus, loving him makes her a potential target for his enemies. When Ellena is kidnapped, Kamran is forced to bring in the Kings.

In the race against time to rescue his woman and defeat his enemies, the kingdom of Durabia will never be the same.

Visit https://books2read.com/Kingofdurabia
to download your copy.

Chaz Maharaj is caught between keeping his public image intact and his heart's desires. The connection with Amanda should have ended with that unconditional "hall pass" which led to one night of unbridled passion. When Amanda walked out of his life, it was supposed to be forever. Neither of them could have anticipated fate's plan.

As Chaz tries to pursue a relationship with her, he's faced with obstacles from his ex-wife and a vicious plot that threatens both their love and Amanda's life. With the help of the Kings of the Castle, Chaz must navigate the treacherous waters of love and deception to protect his newfound love and find a way to be together forever.

Will their love be strong enough to withstand the challenges ahead, or will they be torn apart by forces beyond their control?

https://books2read.com/Knightofbronzeville

When the Kings of the Castle recommend Calvin Atwood, strategic defense inventor, to create a security shield for the kingdom of Durabia, it's the opportunity of a lifetime. The only problem—it's a two-year assignment and he promised his fiancée they would step away from their dangerous lifestyle and start a family.

Security specialist, Mia Jakob, adores Calvin with all her heart, but his last assignment put both of their lives at risk. She understands how important this new role is to the man she loves, but the thought that he may be avoiding commitment does cross her mind.

Calvin was sure he'd made the best decision for his and Mia's future, until enemies of the state target his invention and his woman. Set on a collision course with hidden foes, this Knight will need the help of the Kings to save both his Queen and the Kingdom of Durabia.

https://books2read.com/KnightofSouthHolland

Blair Swanson never expected to find love while on a temporary assignment in the Kingdom of Durabia. But when she meets Hassan, the kingdom's most eligible bachelor, sparks fly between them. Despite his duty to marry for political reasons, Hassan finds himself drawn to the practical and courageous American nurse.

As their feelings for each other deepen, a dark secret threatens to tear them apart. Hassan is torn between his duty to the throne and his love for Blair. With their future hanging in the balance, Blair and Hassan must navigate the complexities of love and duty in a world where nothing is as it seems. Can he find a way to save the woman he loves and fulfill his royal obligations?

Join Blair and Hassan on their journey of love, sacrifice, and discovering what truly matters in Lady of Jeffrey Manor, a heart-warming romance novel that will leave you swooning.

https://books2read.com/Ladyofjefferymanor

Someone is killing women and the villain's next target strikes too close to the Kingdom of Durabia.

Dorian "Ryan" Bostwick is a protector and he's one of the best in the business. When a King of the Castle assigns him to find his former lover, Aziza, he stumbles upon a deadly underworld operating close to the Durabian border.

Aziza Hampton had just rekindled her love affair with Ryan when a night out with friends ends in her kidnapping. Alone and scared, she must find a way to escape her captor and reunite with her lover.

In a race against time, Ryan and the Kings of the Castle follow ominous clues into the underbelly of a system designed to take advantage of the vulnerable. Failure isn't an option and Ryan will rain down hell on earth to save the woman of his heart.

http://books2read.com/KOPI

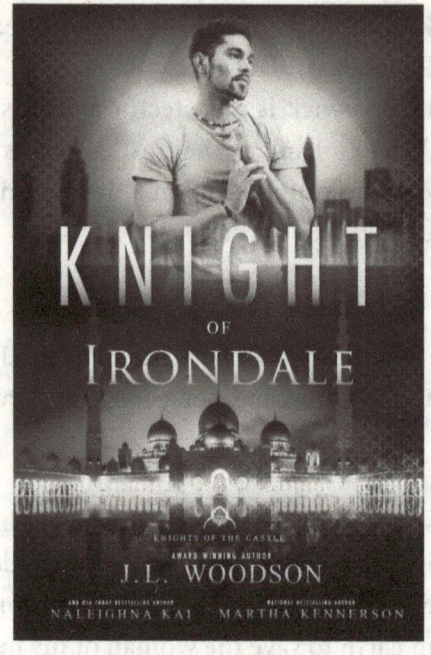

Neesha Carpenter is running from her stalker ex-boyfriend, but now the police have named her the prime suspect in his shooting. With her life in danger and everything spinning out of control, she runs into her high school sweetheart, Christian Vidal, and turns to him for help.

Christian has always been drawn to Neesha's strength, intelligence, and beauty, and he offers her safe haven in the kingdom of Durabia, protecting her from both the danger of her ex and the accusations against her. He enlists the help of the Kings of the Castle to keep her safe, but as their rekindled romance heats up, mounting evidence points to Neesha's guilt. Meanwhile, Neesha's stay in the country puts the royal family at odds with the American government.

As Christian tries to uncover the truth and clear Neesha's name, he

must confront the hard question: did the woman he loves pull the trigger, or is she being framed?
https://books2read.com/Knightofirondale

Rahm Fosten is finally free after serving time for a crime he didn't commit. His priority is taking care of the women who supported him during his hellish journey, and pursuing a relationship with Marilyn Spears. But as he tries to settle into his dream life as a Knight of the Castle, old enemies are waiting in the shadows. An unexpected twist threatens to tear Rahm and Marilyn apart just as they are finally together.

Meanwhile, Rahm's Aunt Alyssa travels to Durabia and catches the eye of Ahmad Maharaj, a wealthy surgeon who is on the cutting edge of the medical industry. But attending a private Bliss event puts her in danger and under the watchful eye of a deadly enemy.

As Rahm and Marilyn navigate their romance, they must also protect their loved ones from a vengeful adversary. The Kings of the Castle are on high alert, ready to do whatever it takes to keep Marilyn, Alyssa, and Rahm's family safe.

Join Rahm and Marilyn on their journey of love and danger in Knight of Grand Crossing, and Alyssa and Ahmad in this heart-pounding international suspense novel

https://books2read.com/Knightofgrandcrossing

Single mothers who are eligible for release, have totally disappeared from the Alabama justice system.Women's advocate, Meghan Turner, has uncovered a disturbing pattern and she's desperate for help. Then her worse nightmare becomes a horrific reality when her friend goes missing under the same mysterious circumstances.

Rory Tannous has spent his life helping society's most vulnerable. When he learns of Meghan's dilemma, he takes it personal. Rory has his own tragic past and he'll utilize every connection, even the King of the Castle, to help this intriguing woman find her friend and the other women.

As Rory and Meghan work together, the attraction grows and so does the danger. The stakes are high and they will have to risk their love and lives to defeat a powerful adversary.

https://books2read.com/Knightofbirmingham2

Following an undercover FBI sting operation that didn't go as planned, Agent Mateo Lopez is ready to put the government agency in his rearview mirror.

A confirmed workaholic, his career soared at the cost of his love life which had crashed and burned until mutual friends arranged a date with beautiful, sharp-witted, Rachel Jordan, a rising star at a children's social services agency.

Unlucky in love, Rachel has sworn off romantic relationships, but Mateo finds himself falling for her in more ways than one. When trouble brews in one of Rachel's cases, he does everything in his power to keep her safe—even if it means resorting to extreme measures.

Will the choices they make bring them closer together or cost them their lives?

https://books2read.com/Knight-of-Penn-Quarter

QUEENS OF THE CASTLE SERIES

ABOUT THE QUEENS OF THE CASTLE SERIES
Each Queen book is a standalone, without cliffhangers
USA TODAY, and National Bestselling Authors have created a world where women can—and will have it all—love, family, career, and leave a legacy while overcoming generational challenges.

Someone is sabotaging Dr. Lani Jamison's career and their tactics are escalating. Are the attacks attempts to prevent Lani from working with The Castle to implement robotic surgery in the hospital? Or does her association with Jordan Spears have his clients seeking to take her out of the picture?

Jordan lives a complicated life from his family dynamics to his "interesting" career.When Lani tries to distance herself from him, he's forced to temporarily accept it as he staves off the hostile demands of his brother who has racked up debt with the criminals who won't take no for an answer. Will Jordan be able to convince Lani that their relationship deserves a chance despite its origins? And will Lani survive an unknown enemy's endeavor to put her six feet under?

https://books2read.com/QueenofLahaina

Not all monsters are born, some are made.

Killing Carpathia was the first mistake. Informing her niece made it worse. Durabia meant a fresh start for Raye Bennett. One phone call destroyed all of that. Returning to American soil could send her back to prison for the rest of her life. Attending the funeral of a family member may be deadlier. Heaven and Hell change places in this romantic thriller where the poison is sweeter than the wine.

https://books2read.com/QueenofShadowBay

Solange Porter never believed her husband, Emeril would betray her. But he did. First, he died when he promised they'd be together forever. Then, he left her as the head of a tech company that she didn't want to lead. She wasn't alone; most of the staff felt the same way.

Computer programmer Wale Adisa needs Solange's help. To get it, he will share a secret that Emeril never revealed to her. This secret will not only increase her feelings of betrayal. It may also place a target on her back that could ruin her and the company she's trying to save.

https://books2read.com/Queenofnorthshore

By birth, she is royalty. By choice she is an avenger and equalizer for those who have no voice. When dark forces emerge and threaten not only her queendom but her life, Luiza, Queen of Belize becomes a foot soldier, calling upon the assistance of allies and a few nemeses to help aid in a personal war. It's then that she fulfills the meaning of her name, glorious war hero.

https://books2read.com/Queenofbahia

Samantha DaCosta, reporter extraordinaire, stumbles upon an explosive story in her research of several wealthy, humanitarians connected to The Castle, a place reserved for the mega-rich.

Her uncle, who is a member, has invested in a medical facility that produces and distributes vaccines to third-world countries. The medication has deadly adverse effects, which sets up Ted DaCosta as a target for blackmail.

As Sam uncovers disturbing details, she's conflicted. When her personal safety is threatened, she must either pretend not to know the implications of this nefarious plot, or speak up and bring down a hailstorm of publicity. Danger also stalks her to Jamaica in the form of an assassination attempt.

Kingston "King" Coburn is content to support his woman's endeavors, but when work impacts her well-being, he draws the line. Instead of pulling her back from the edge of a dark abyss, he's drawn into the world of power brokers, who will do anything to increase their wealth.

Only the couple's combined skills and access to a safe haven will keep them alive at the end of their harrowing search for the truth.
https://books2read.com/Queen-of-Kingston

QUEEN OF CAMBRIDGE

Billionaire chocolatier Caressa Sidaná is one of the most recognizable names in the confectionery industry, but she is looking to expand into other ventures.

She is shrewd and no-nonsense, but in her pursuit of business dominance, she has made some mistakes along the way, including the oft-clichéd misstep of mixing business with pleasure.

Her expansion efforts lead to a chance meeting with Ishmael Abdur-Hafiz, an international weapons dealer with the type of connections that could prove beneficial for all parties involved. Their intense attraction and mutual business pursuits draw the attention of a former lover-turned-enemy, intent on ruining everything she has built and permanently removing Ishmael from her life.

Can she find a way to deal with the consequences of her decisions and save her company from potential destruction?

https://books2read.com/Queen-of-Cambridge

Milan Alessia Jackson battled through the scars left in her life from a contentious relationship. Her grandaunt served as her protector and guardian angel until she took her last breath. International lawyer Vikkas Germaine was her childhood friend and true love. Life's circumstances separated them, but his father served as the catalyst to reunite them.

As the couple settle into their new marriage and Durabia, unexpected challenges rise up and threaten to tear their relationship apart. Secrets from her past, an unexpected trip to South Carolina and family members primed to settle scores surface, leading to a whirlwind of upheaval in their lives. Can their love survive these storms or will forces in play destroy everything they're building?

https://books2read.com/QueenofWilmette

Waking up from a coma—without her memory intact—is not something Cassandra anticipated when she says her goodbyes to her best friend, promising to find her daughter, along with the other children who went missing since the arrival of an unknown criminal organization in Curaçao.

https://books2read.com/Queencuracao

Someone is tampering with the water supply in the small Brazilian community, causing many to get sick, including Pilár Silva's beloved grandmother. Pilár leaves Chicago and travels to Salvador, Bahia at the start of Carnival season. She must trust Yoshi Tanaka's expertise as a scientist and his abilities to keep her safe.

Yoshi, an award-winning Hydrologist, is supposed to stay in Rio for a conference, but he honors his brother's request to help a coworker from The Castle who's in the region. In order to keep Pilár safe, he must keep her close.

Danger stalks them like a thief in the night. Will they explore their budding feelings, or will one of them end up in a shallow grave?
https://books2read.com/Queenofbahia

ABOUT KAREN D. BRADLEY

National bestselling author, Karen D. Bradley has penned several contemporary fiction and suspense novels. She has also contributed short stories to the Sugar anthology and the Just One Kiss anthology. Venturing into film making, she wrote and produced a short film based on one of her novels. Visit Karen on the web at www.karendbradley.com

Join her mailing list: https://landing.mailerlite.com/webforms/landing/p2l5h5

Printed in the USA
CPSIA information can be obtained
at www.ICGtesting.com
CBHW011916051124
16954CB00009B/130

9 781733 608978